"Need S

The deeply voiced offer ~~~~~~~~ car window.

A tough-looking face was only inches away from hers. Her peripheral vision took in an extremely stubborn looking chin, hazed by golden stubble. Above it was a mouth that twisted into a crooked grin at her examination, and a nose that looked as though it might have pushed its way into more than one unpleasant situation.

But it was the eyes that did it. Deep-set, hazel, surrounded by a thicket of bronze-colored lashes, they were the wickedest eyes she'd ever seen—and amazingly enough, the warmest.

She shook her head and he wheeled his motorcycle off, seeming to be a part of his mount, like some modern-day centaur.

═══════════════════════════════════

DIXIE BROWNING

is a native of North Carolina, and many of her stories are born as she travels from her home in Winston-Salem to her cottage in Frisco, on Hatteras Island. She is also an accomplished watercolor artist, as well as a writer.

Dear Reader:

SILHOUETTE DESIRE is an exciting new line of contemporary romances from Silhouette Books. During the past year, many Silhouette readers have written in telling us what other types of stories they'd like to read from Silhouette, and we've kept these comments and suggestions in mind in developing SILHOUETTE DESIRE.

DESIREs feature all of the elements you like to see in a romance, plus a more sensual, provocative story. So if you want to experience all the excitement, passion and joy of falling in love, then SILHOUETTE DESIRE is for you.

For more details write to:

Jane Nicholls
Silhouette Books
PO Box 236
Thornton Road
Croydon
Surrey CR9 3RU

DIXIE BROWNING
The Tender Barbarian

Silhouette Desire
Originally Published by Silhouette Books
division of
Harlequin Enterprises Ltd.

First published in Great Britain 1985
by Mills & Boon Ltd, 15–16 Brook's Mews, London W1A 1DR

© Dixie Browning 1985

Silhouette, Silhouette Desire and Colophon are Trade Marks of Harlequin Enterprises B.V.

ISBN 0 373 05188 3

22-0885

Made and printed in Great Britain by
Richard Clay (The Chaucer Press) Ltd,
Bungay, Suffolk

Other Silhouette Books by Dixie Browning

Silhouette Desire

Shadow of Yesterday
Image of Love
The Hawk and the Honey
Late Rising Moon
Stormwatch

Silhouette Special Edition

Finders Keepers
Reach Out to Cherish
Just Deserts
Time and Tide

*For further information about
Silhouette Books please write to:*

Jane Nicholls
Silhouette Books
PO Box 236
Thornton Road
Croydon
Surrey CR9 3RU

The Tender Barbarian

1

To bed her, or not to bed her," Beyard Jones muttered thoughtfully. *"That* is the question."

After due consideration, he abstained. Three short paragraphs later he typed "THE END" and ripped the page from the battered portable, only five days past his contractual deadline. A single well-documented consummation and a few near-misses would have to do it this time. When he'd first started out, writing steamy love scenes had been a real turn-on, but by the time his fourth book had gone into its fifth printing, he'd found it more boring than stimulating. Possibly because he'd been so damned busy writing about it he'd had too little time to engage in any firsthand experiences.

Some forty-five minutes later, as he settled a vi-sored helmet over his thatch of sun-streaked hair, it occurred to him that he was going to be busier than ever for the next few months. Just as well he'd fulfilled his current contract. He'd allow himself a week's break, another week to come up with a decent proposal, and then he'd drag out contract negotiations for a couple more weeks before putting himself into another deadline situation.

Touching the bulky padded envelope in his motorcycle's saddlebag, he turned on the quiet BMW R75 and headed for the post office to mail the manuscript. That done, he'd be on his way out of town. With any luck, he'd beat the evening traffic across the Bay Bridge.

Taking the Ritchie highway south from Baltimore, Bey flexed his shoulder muscles. Speed-induced wind whipped faded jeans against his thick leather boots, reddened a twice-broken nose and a chin that still sported a few ancient battle scars. Tough, compactly constructed, Bey Jones had come up the hard way. It showed.

By the time he turned off on 50-301, some of the strain of the past few weeks had already begun to ease. As he neared the bridge, breathing in the pungent bay air, a few of the lines that added premature age to his weathered face began to smooth out.

Those last two chapters had been killers. As usual, he'd found himself smoking nonstop, existing on beer, black coffee and Vienna sausage while he worked the clock around to gather up all the threads he'd cast onto the loom of the story and weave them into a tight, satisfying ending.

It didn't get any better. He'd thought that after all these years the process of writing would grow easier. It hadn't worked out that way. The more he wrote, the more he learned of his craft, the higher his standards grew. According to the reviews, each of his five published romances had surpassed the one before, and every one of them had made it to a respectable rung on the best-seller lists—which added a subtle pressure all its own.

It had been his accountant who'd insisted that he incorporate himself. The fact that he even needed an accountant still took some getting used to. From the tender age of eleven, he'd worked his tail off for every dime he'd ever had. Now, at thirty-two, he was a corporation, a property owner, and weather permitting, soon to become a home owner.

The quiet purr of the well-bred street bike throbbed between his powerful thighs as he leaned into the wind. Fletcher's Landing—*his*. He'd first seen the wooded peninsula from the bay, from the cockpit of the rugged work boat he'd bought, repaired and renamed the *Bonnie Bonus*. She'd been running rough ever since he'd left Baltimore, and he'd finally headed her for the nearest lea shore to change the plugs. It had been exactly one year ago. The trees had been incandescent with color against the somber darkness of the river. Tucked away from the raw winds of the open bay, he'd anchored near the ruins of an ancient wharf.

It had caught at his imagination. He'd gone ashore and explored, looking for some sign of habitation, finding none. The following weekend he'd left the *Bonus* at home and taken the bike. He'd had a hell of a time locating the place from the highway, but he'd finally found it. Aside from a small frame house practically straddling the narrow neck of the peninsula, it was uninhabited.

He'd spent that weekend and many more camping in a secluded cove as far from the house as possible. If the place was posted, he'd missed the signs—but then, he hadn't wasted much time looking for them.

Through the double blind of a Baltimore realtor and his corporation, Bon-Bey, Inc., he'd made an offer for the place, hardly daring to hope he'd be successful. He'd wanted the whole thing—a place where he could relax and be himself without worrying about having his privacy invaded. Never gregarious, he'd grown positively reclusive since his first romance novel had hit the top. He could count on the fingers of one hand the people who knew of his identity as Bonnie Jericho, and that was five people too many.

According to the realtor, the owner wouldn't part with the cottage, but he'd managed to secure all but the few acres immediately surrounding it. It was the first time in his life he'd owned anything more valuable than the bike, the boat and a portable typewriter. Even now, it scared the hell out of him.

A hollow belly reminded him that he'd been in too big a hurry to get out of Baltimore to eat, much less to pack provisions. He pulled into a convenience store in Easton and stocked up on crackers, chocolate bars, Vienna sausage, sardines, beer and marshmallows. It should get him through the weekend. If not, he could always run into St. Michaels for a meal or two.

Emily McCloud gripped the steering wheel and made a deliberate effort to unwind. In spite of all the years she'd spent getting her teaching degree and securing a post at Eastwood Academy, it would take about one more week like this last one had been to make her chuck the whole bundle. What on earth had induced her to think she'd find fulfillment in introducing to a group of boy-crazy teenagers the joys of English literature?

She ground the starter again and swore with a fluency that would have sent generations of distaff McClouds into a spin. Her car hated damp weather. It started on the fourth try, and Emily left the faculty parking area and waited for an opening in the late-afternoon traffic. It was beginning to drizzle, and she had a round of errands to do—and unless she could get her mind back on track again, she'd probably forget half of them.

Her high, pale forehead furrowed gently above a pair of dark, silky eyebrows. It wasn't enough that all the faculty and staff had to take a cut in pay. It wasn't enough that the radiator in her room was manic-depressive. Since the first day of the term she'd been fighting the pernicious influence of those paperback romances that were handed around the class until they were falling apart, and today had been no better. If she were to give a pop quiz on Devereaux and Dailey and Jericho, her class would ace it, but Steinbeck? According to Mollie Crandall, he was a baseball player!

The rumors of impending bankruptcy had been officially denied again today. She'd dropped by the staff lounge to see if she could glean anything from the gossip mill, and discovered Abbie Linga, the headmistress, lying down with her feet up, her shoes off, and a box of chocolates on her flat stomach. She'd been steaming her glasses over the latest torrid paperback. Emily had turned and walked out again.

"Hang in there, McCloud," she grumbled, edging into a tight parking slot. "A weekend of peace and

quiet will cure what ails you." She corrected herself;
make that one hour of peace and quiet and thirty-five
hours of grading test papers, reading things she had
no interest in reading, and then grinding out her
weekly book review. For the weekly pittance.

The first stop was the *Talbot Light,* to drop off her
copy and collect the books for next week's reviews.
After that, she'd pick up her coat from the cleaner—
then go by the hardware store and the grocer's—if she
could find her list.

She was simply going to have to ask Wendell for
another column; two pittances would be better than
one. The trouble was, she wasn't an expert in anything, except possibly teenage girls and modern
literature—and she was beginning to doubt her expertise even there.

It would have to be something special to entice
Wendell to give her more space. In all the years she'd
known him, including the two years she'd been
engaged to him, she'd never known him to let his
personal interests interfere with business. Not that she
was of interest to him personally now, except as an old
friend.

Bracing herself a few minutes later, she lifted her
chin and opened the door marked Managing Editor.
"Wendell, if you have a minute, I'd like to talk to you,"
she announced briskly.

In the moment before he acknowledged her presence, Emily studied Wendell Twiford objectively. The
hair that had once been stove-polish black was now
well shot with silver, and not even the tinted horn-
rimmed glasses could hide the pouches beneath his
pale blue eyes. It had been . . . Lord, it had been

seventeen years since he'd given her the small solitaire.

Removing his glasses, Wendell glanced up at the tall dark-haired woman before him. "Hello, Em. How's school these days?"

"Don't ask. I only hope I get something better to read this weekend than I did last time. Stream-of-consciousness babbling from a paranoid prisoner isn't exactly my idea of weekend entertainment. If he ever reads my review, he'll know for sure the system's out to get him."

"Call 'em as you see 'em, Miss Emily. You wanted to talk to me?"

"Wendell, I have an idea for a new column. You remember that syndicated thing on gourmet dining we ran several years back? It was pretty popular, wasn't it? I could do a weekly column on gracious dining—menu, recipes, wines—maybe even flowers and suitable dinner music." Her voice grew vibrant as eagerness brushed the subtle hollows of her cheeks with color. "I'm talking about a dining-room piece, Wendell —not just another kitchen column."

"Candlelight and wine?" Wendell's voice was dry as he lifted a brow in amusement. "Don't tell me you've finally discovered romance, Em."

"I'm talking about civilized dining as opposed to burgers and fries," Emily snapped. "And don't mention romance to me, please. At the moment my tolerance is paper-thin!"

"So what else is new?" Wendell jeered softly.

"Wendell, I'm not in the mood for your sarcasm. My head aches, I've got a stack of test papers to grade and a list of errands to run before I can go home."

"I'm sorry, hon—just teasing. Want to go to the club dance tomorrow night?"

"With three books to review, a stack of papers to grade and the storm windows to put up? Hardly."

Emily knew exactly how to interpret the invitation. The family membership had never been renewed after her parents' death, but now and then Wendell offered to escort her, along with his own date, out of consideration for the fact that they'd known each other all their lives.

He needn't have bothered. Emily's social life had withered and died except for an occasional movie or a concert with someone from the school. There simply wasn't time for more, but she hadn't really missed it.

At the moment she almost resented Wendell's kindness. The trouble was, they knew each other too well. Their families had always been friends, and they'd drifted into an engagement that had weathered her first year at the university and Wendell's struggle to get a moribund publishing firm on its feet again. But after the tragedy, when she'd had to take over the raising of her two younger sisters, it had been strained beyond the limit. Wendell had insisted she make other arrangements for the girls, and she'd refused. The engagement had ended with all the excitement of a wet firecracker.

"What about it, Wendell? I thought Friday would be a good day." Need battled with pride as Emily tried her best to sound unconcerned.

"Emily, the appeal is too limited. Stick to your book reviews and your schoolteaching, hmm? At the moment I'm doing my damnedest to make room for a travel feature beginning the first of the year."

Emily's level gray eyes flared to brightness and then

faded again. She'd have loved tackling something like that, but unless it would support her—and small columns for a small daily wouldn't—she couldn't give up her teaching. Unless it gave her up first. "Who's doing it?"

"Nancy. She's on a cruise right now—which is why I asked about the dance. If you want to go, I'll take you."

Nancy Roscoe was blond and petite and divorced, and she'd had her eye on Wendell since junior-high-school days. Emily stood and brushed a hand down her wool paisley skirt. "No thanks, Wendell. I'm booked solid all weekend." With characteristic self-honesty, she admitted that she resented Nancy Roscoe's getting the travel column more than she did her finally getting Wendell.

"I heard you sold the Landing, Em. Why don't you take the money and treat yourself to a cruise? Nancy could put you onto some decent ones—you might even get a reservation on the Love Boat." His grin was only slightly mocking, but it was enough to send a hot rush of color to Emily's cheeks.

"Wendell, did anyone ever tell you—"

"You did, Em—frequently."

"Well, double it—in spades!"

"Don't forget to pick up the books on your way out," he reminded her calmly, reaching for a stack of papers in an obvious gesture of dismissal.

By the time she got outside, Emily had cooled off. Why did she let Wendell's remarks get under her skin? He hadn't wanted her enough to share the burden of her family at a time when she'd really needed him, and, Lord knows, she'd long since got over any damage to her heart.

At the hardware store Emily bought another gallon of paint for the shutters. The price had risen since the gallon she'd bought only last spring. She walked briskly to her next stop on the same block, only to discover that the dry cleaner couldn't locate her coat. Shifting his cigar, he asked her to describe it.

"It's a beige vicuna polo coat," Emily said irritably, failing to add that it was seventeen years old and had been relined three times. It was still a good coat.

"Reg'lar girl's off this week. Check back later."

Two doors down was a convenience store. She could pick up a few items there and skip the grocer's. Emily stood on the sidewalk considering which to save—time or money. There was a motorcycle squeezed in the space in front of her car. Desperately needing a scapegoat, she told herself that unless the owner moved it within thirty seconds he was going to be sorry. The bike was in better condition than her old sedan—a little scraped paint wouldn't bother her at all. In fact, she'd welcome the chance to grind something other than her teeth!

She ground the starter. The thing groaned impotently, and Emily swore under her breath. She felt an absurd desire to bury her face in her hands and cry—which would solve precisely nothing.

"Need some help?"

The deeply voiced offer came clearly through the one-inch crack of her window, and Emily turned to see a leather-covered arm bracing itself on her door. Her startled glance shot upward to a tough-looking face, the eyes glinting only inches away from hers. Her peripheral vision took in a chin—an extremely stubborn-looking chin, hazed by a golden stubble that

18

failed to disguise two small scars. Above it was a mouth that responded to her unconscious examination by twisting into a crooked grin. Whether friendly or mocking, she couldn't have said. The confrontation took place in mere moments—moments in which she had time to notice a nose that looked as though it might have pushed its way into more than one unpleasant situation.

It was the eyes that did it. Deep-set, hazel, surrounded by a thicket of bronze-colored lashes, they were the wickedest eyes she'd ever seen—and amazingly enough, the warmest.

Disconcerted, she blurted something that couldn't possibly have been heard through the glass. She twisted the key once more, and this time the engine coughed into life. Her eyes still entangled in a compelling thicket of bronze and green and amber, Emily watched the man back away and turn toward the motorcycle. Her hand on the gear lever, she waited until he'd mounted the sheepskin-covered seat. One booted foot on the curb, he tossed a quick grin over his shoulder and then wheeled off into the street, his muscular body leaning with the angle of his mount like some modern-day centaur.

Emily remembered to shop for the week's groceries, then drove halfway home without them and had to go back. By the time she pulled up beside the cottage it was dark, and a cold, despondent drizzle had set in.

After a hastily prepared dinner, eaten on a mahogany table that was far too large for the small room, on china that had been in her family for generations, Emily braced herself to begin her required reading. She never read at the table. She couldn't allow herself to backslide into careless habits, living alone as she did. There were standards to be maintained, and once she began letting down her guard, she'd be lost.

Carefully she washed and dried and put away the Wedgwood and rock crystal. She spread the linen towel on the rack, lotioned her hands, and went into the cluttered living room. Then, with only the smallest sigh, she reached for the first book. She hadn't even checked to see what she was in for this weekend.

A new release, it was fairly good, but even though her headache was under control, her concentration was shot. She kept seeing a vision of hazel eyes and an impudent grin in a face that was, for all its battered irregularities, compellingly attractive.

At ten she gave up and reached for the stack of test papers. While rain drummed sullenly on the metal roof, she skimmed the answers and made her marks. Finally, yawning widely, she stood up and stretched. Cocoa and bed—she'd finish the tests tomorrow. It was going to be too wet to paint shutters and put up storm windows, anyway.

After making herself a cup of cocoa, she prowled restlessly through the house. It was hopelessly over-crowded. Sometimes she wished she had the nerve to cart it all off to a junk dealer and start fresh, but she knew she'd regret it. This was all she had now that both girls were married and living so far away. Neither Vangie nor Libby had wanted any of the McCloud furniture. She'd sold the really good pieces, splitting the money three ways. She'd kept only the white elephants. The Victorian pump organ with the asthmatic bellows, the miserable old satin-striped Biedermeier sofa, the breakfront with the missing pediment—they were family things, imbued with memories of her earliest childhood, when her grandparents were still alive. Even her bedroom was taken up by an enormous sleigh bed that was valueless because it had once been damaged and clumsily repaired.

More than once she'd made up her mind to chuck it all and leave Maryland, to try to enjoy what was left of her youth before it was too late, but at the last minute she always backed out. She'd already used up her youth, and as for moving—dammit, she'd retrenched as far as she intended to.

Four generations of McClouds had lived in Talbot County, the earliest of them, Fletcher McCloud, making a modest fortune in shipping. They'd built up an estate that included a three-story colonial home near Easton that was now listed with the Maryland Historical Trust, and much later, the small cottage at Fletcher's Landing, a wooded peninsula near St. Michaels.

Holmes McCloud, Emily's father, had been an impractical dreamer and an alcoholic. What was left of a once proud shipping company, originally built around a splendid fleet of rams and schooners, had never quite made it into the age of computerized, containerized shipping. Under Holmes's incompetent directorship, it had finally sunk without a trace.

The Easton house had gone next, during Emily's last year of high school. She'd been in her first year at the university when her father's fatal heart attack had occurred. She'd dropped out, knowing that her mother would have her hands full with the two afterthoughts, as Holmes and Ansie McCloud had called their two youngest daughters, born nine and ten years after Emily.

Two days after Holmes's funeral, Ansie took the

week's dose of sleeping pills she'd been given to get her through the shock of losing her husband so suddenly. It had been totally unexpected, if only because Holmes's and Ansie's marriage had been one continuous polite battle, fought with saccharine words and poisonous looks.

Emily had moved herself and her two young sisters out of the expensive apartment her parents had leased and into the Fletcher's Landing cottage, over the vociferous protests of both girls. She'd taken them out of Eastwood Academy, where three generations of McCloud women had studied, and had enrolled them in the public school.

Eventually, Vangie had married a California fruit grower, and Libby, the younger by some thirteen months, had met and married the son of a French diplomat and was presently living in Paris.

In and between and around the bringing up of her two sisters, Emily had managed to complete her own education, switching her major from art to a more practical field.

She'd hung onto Fletcher's Landing as long as she could, loving the deep, shadowy woods with their earthy, resinous smell, and the soothing sound of lapping waters around the ruins of an ancient wharf. It had been her refuge, her haven, the balm that had healed the surface wounds of day-to-day living. It had helped assuage the deeper ones that had come with the gradual realization that from a high point that had not been all that high, her life had begun a slow, gentle decline, and there was no reason to believe it would ever climb again.

The unexpected offer had been too good to turn down. With the three school loans to pay off, and two weddings to finish paying for, she'd been severely strapped. But she'd refused to sell the cottage. She'd kept the few acres immediately surrounding her house, and given instead a right-of-way onto the peninsula through her land. She'd split the money three ways, using her share to pay off her debts.

On Monday morning she was awakened by the sound of a vehicle passing her house. After striding to the front porch in her gown and slippers and seeing no one, she sighed and went inside again. It was hard to get over a feeling of possessiveness toward the land her family had owned for so long, but Fletcher's Landing was no longer her responsibility. If trespassers invaded it, leaving their litter behind, it was up to the new owners to put a stop to it. Hunters and fishermen had ignored the "No Trespassing" signs for years, and someone had been sneaking in to camp for the past year.

A feeling of unfocused resentment persisted, and Emily entered Wendell's office the following afternoon with an aggressive burst of energy that brought her skirts swirling about her long, shapely legs.

"Read 'em and weep," she pronounced defiantly as she placed her copy on Wendell's desk. "Since when did we dignify trash with a review?" Her fists on her hips, she dug her knuckles defiantly into the soft wool knit of the mulberry-colored pullover as she waited for an answer.

"Trash?" Wendell responded absently, running his finger down a long column in a word estimate that would be accurate to within six words.

"The Bonnie Jericho thing. Tell me, Wendell, do women actually swallow that tripe?"

"Oh, the romance." His voice was dry, his eyes amused. "Jericho's a best-seller—supposed to be regional. And why ask me what women read?" he dismissed, returning his gaze to the page before him.

Emily snorted in disgust, and Wendell looked up again, his finger anchoring a word to the newsprint. "I suppose I should have known better than to ask you to read the romance," he said wearily. "You know, you continue to amaze me, Em—you could be a beautiful woman if you bothered to make the effort, but your nose is getting slightly out of shape from being pressed to that self-imposed grindstone of yours."

The arrow found its target, but a slatelike opacity disguised the hurt in Emily's dark gray eyes. "In case you've forgotten, the grindstone was hardly self-imposed. Besides, you had your own particular grindstone, remember?" The demands of an ailing newspaper had been Wendell's argument against taking on the burden of a ready-made family.

"I haven't forgotten. At least I knew better than to allow a grindstone to become a millstone around my neck."

"Well, bully for you."

Wendell shook his head mockingly. "You could never get beyond this stage of a discussion without falling back on a cliché, could you, Em? For an English teacher your vocabulary is remarkably limited."

Emily took a deep, calming breath. She'd long since learned to deal with Wendell's taunts. "Not as limited as you might think," she purred, eyes still stony. "Maybe you'd better have your lawyer go over the book reviews before Tuesday. If Miss Jericho should happen to see a copy of our modest little rag, you're probably going to hear from her." With that she swung around and strode to the door, back rigid, head held high under a burden of rich chestnut-brown hair.

Wendell's reminder to pick up the next batch of books on her way out somewhat dampened the effect of her exit line, and she whispered an oath as she veered off to collect two spy thrillers and the biography of a comedian who was notorious for his love affairs.

At least there were no more so-called romances to strain her credulity. At some age, women of even moderate intelligence were supposed to get over believing in Prince Charming and knights in shining armor. Lord knows, after growing up in a household where the kindest words spoken between her parents was apt to be "please pass the salt," she hadn't expected to be whirled away on a cloud of moon madness, but even so, she'd been disappointed. Her engagement had been a farce, and the two later relationships she'd almost ventured into had reaffirmed her belief that men were takers, not givers—not even sharers.

Bey tried the door again, and then walked around to the back of the small frame house that all but blocked access to his property. The realtor had said she wouldn't budge, but it wouldn't hurt to give it one more try. According to what he'd been able to learn, the woman was the last of an old, once prominent Eastern Shore family, a spinster who'd dug herself in after selling off everything but her home.

Lord knows, Bey could sympathize with her for

wanting to hang in there. If he'd ever had a genuine home, he might not be so all-fired bent on what he was doing.

"Lady, you've got what I want, and I'm just mean enough to go after it," he muttered, eyeing the peeling paint on the back of the house. The poor old creature couldn't even look after what she had. She'd be much better off in a retirement home or one of those cubbyholes designed for elderly singles.

He'd pay her twice what it was worth—hell, he'd already paid her enough for the rest of her land to gold-plate this place. Maybe she was one of those cranks who hoarded it all away in a shoebox. Maybe she'd endowed a home for cats. Bingo games? The horses? Could be. At any rate, he rationalized half-guiltily, he'd be doing her a favor to get her out of here and into town where someone responsible could look after her.

"Hey, anybody home?" he called out, pounding on the dark green front door one last time. At least she'd taken the trouble to spruce up the front of the house—shutters in good shape, windows sparkling. And gutters full of leaves and pinestraw, he noted as he backed down the single step and out onto the autumn-littered brick walk that led out to the narrow rutted road.

Straddling the BMW again, Bey headed for town. It was too wet to camp out. Dammit, he hated having to spend a single minute of his precious free time shut up in the impersonal walls of a motel. Once he'd made up his mind, he'd been so eager to get on with the building that he'd overcome the contractor's objections by agreeing to hire two crews to get the place under way before winter set in. He'd located the corners today, and left the men putting up batter boards.

The thought of owning his own home had grown like a fever in him. Dim memories of the only home he could remember had long since been overlaid with the series of institutions he'd known since his mother had dumped him in the lap of the state authorities. If she'd actually been his real mother; he'd never been sure. Fortunately, he'd learned survival skills fast.

Dining alone in the motel restaurant on fried oysters, Bey considered the unlikely route that had brought him to the brink of taxpaying respectability. It had been the books that had been his salvation. The sporadic education he'd picked up had introduced him to the western classics. On his own, he'd read everything Zane Gray and Louis L'Amour had ever written, and by the time he was old enough to enlist in the army he'd written three bad westerns.

It had taken him a long time to figure out just why they were so bad, but he'd done it. The trouble was, he'd never met a horse face to face in his life, and the closest he'd come to a bunkhouse was an army barracks in Fort Bragg. Hell, he was a waterman. Son of a merchant seaman—at least that was what he'd been told—he'd lived around the bay area all his life, usually one step ahead of one set of authorities or another, depending on his age.

The army had been a blessing to him. Once his initial training had ended, he'd taken every course he could fit into his schedule. By the time he'd got out, he might have earned himself a degree, but he'd audited most courses, wanting the knowledge far more than a piece of paper.

He would have stayed in longer but for a sniper's

bullet that had landed him flat on his back for three months. It was while he was in the V.A. hospital that the local ladies' auxiliary had mixed up their book delivery. Having read everything the skimpy library provided, Bey had grumblingly read his first paperback romance.

By the time he'd finished the lot, he was itching to write again. Dammit, he might not know much about range wars and cattle stampedes, but he knew about women—bad ones, not-so-bad ones, the beautiful and the unbeautiful.

It was almost like a new frontier, with the heroine fighting against overwhelming odds to hang on to her newly won territory. He understood genre books, having spent so much time between the covers of westerns. Romances weren't all that different— variations on a theme, with far more scope than the standard horse-and-gun epic. In the good ones, the writing was superb—witty as well as tender.

Oddly enough, it was the tenderness that appealed to him most of all. It was an exotic new taste on his tongue, an intoxicating new world waiting to be explored. If fantasy was what women wanted, he had a few of his own he'd like to share.

He'd gone back to Baltimore after being discharged, simply because it was familiar. He'd leased a row house that was little more than a tenement and bought himself a portable typewriter from a pawnshop. The advance on his first book barely covered the rent and a few supplies, but he'd gotten a nibble on a second book, and with that under his belt, he'd signed on with an agent.

His next advance was considerably more than he'd expected, even minus the agent's cut. With it he'd bought himself enough decent clothes to get him through a weekend in New York at contract time, and then he'd bought his first yacht. Much in need of repairs, the twenty-seven-foot oyster boat was unremarkable on the outside, which suited him just fine. His defensive instincts were too well-developed for ostentation, even now that he could afford it. Flash it around, and you get it ripped off. Blend in, and you stand a chance of surviving. Those were among the earliest lessons he'd learned.

He'd blended in. Over the next few years, as his bank balance had soared to numbing heights, he'd learned his way around a different jungle. He could hold his own on any turf, from New York's Upper East Side to Baltimore's slums. The purchase of Fletcher's Landing had leveled his funds considerably, but with the delivery fee for his last manuscript he'd have more than enough to build the sort of house he had in mind.

Back in his motel room again after the indigestible meal, Bey prowled, pausing now and then to stare out into the courtyard with the covered swimming pool. He waited until there was no one in sight and then he turned up his collar and dashed out into the rain. Minutes later he wheeled the dripping BMW into his carpeted room. He didn't own much, but what he did own, he damned well knew how to protect.

2

~ccccccccccccc~

The hell you say," Bey growled, lifting his naked back from the pillows. He'd showered and, still damp, had settled onto the bed with a cigar and a copy of the morning paper.

The review had taken him by surprise. If publishers wanted to send out advance copies, that was their privilege. Bey's agent passed on the royalty statements and the checks, and that was all the news he needed to know. After reading one or two articles on romances and the women who wrote them, he'd deliberately turned his back on newsletters, reviews and anything not directly related to his own work.

It was strictly hype—this business of writing in purple satin nightgowns, in lilac-scented bubble baths, and drinking only Dom Pérignon chilled in sterling-silver ice buckets. Bey's sense of privacy was too deeply ingrained to expose himself to that sort of rubbish. It was awkward enough being a man in what was predominantly a woman's realm. Damned if he wanted it bruited about that he wrote his books wearing silk pajama pants and kept a harem for inspiration and research.

Scowling, he allowed his eyes to be drawn once more to the scurrilous attack. "'Victimized females'? Lady, you're nuts!" he grunted. "'Addictive, pernicious pap ladled out ad nauseam by a woman whose tastes obviously became fixed somewhere between late puberty and early adolescence. Miss Jericho is a traitor to her gender.'"

Crushing the paper as he leaned forward, Bey lunged for the notebook and pen that were never far from his side. "If I'm a traitor to your gender, lady, what the devil does that make you?"

Tossing aside the front section of the paper, he smoothed out the offending article and checked the byline. "McCloud? Do I know you from somewhere?" The name had a familiar ring to it. He repeated it aloud and then, shaking his head to clear away the distraction, he began scribbling.

"Miss McCloud . . . who is obviously totally unfamiliar with romance in any form . . ." he mumbled as he wrote, "would do well to curb her vituperative tongue . . . lest she earn the pity of her readers. There is nothing more pathetic . . . than a woman incapable of appreciating her . . . *womanhood!* If my heroine appears . . . victimized to you, Miss McCloud, and my hero overbearing . . . it could be because you have obviously . . . never been made aware of the basic physical differences between the sexes. Not *genders,* Miss McCloud," Bey scribbled angrily. *"Sexes!"*

Appending the ambiguous initials B.J., Bey

searched through the plastic-veneer drawers until he located an envelope bearing the motel's logo. Checking the newspaper's masthead, he addressed it and enclosed the lined page from his notebook. Oblivious of his state of nudity, he crossed the room and laid the letter on the seat of his bike.

Then, stretching out on the bed once more, he crossed his arms under his head, stared up at the rough plaster ceiling and began visualizing the house that would soon be taking shape on the shore of his own stretch of the bay—or more accurately, the mouth of the Miles River.

Reluctantly Emily unrolled the morning paper with one hand while she stirred her coffee. Wendell had phoned the night before to alert her.

"Answer it in Friday's edition, Em," he'd ordered. "This sort of thing is great for circulation. I wouldn't be surprised if we don't generate a few more letters before it runs its course."

"Wendell, I don't write letters to the editor unless I feel it's my civic duty, and this hardly falls into that category. If some woman wants to indulge in a public brawl over a sleazy romance, that's her business. I don't have to be a part of it."

"You *are* a part of it. You landed the first punch with your review, and it was a doozy. I didn't think even you would go that far."

"I warned you when I handed it in—if you didn't like it, you could have killed it. And what do you mean, even me?" She clamped her teeth into a slice of dry toast while she rustled through the paper to find the editorial page.

"Figure of speech, Em—forget it."

"And stop calling me Em! It makes me feel like someone's grandmother!"

Wendell's chuckle came through quite clearly, and Emily visualized those pale blue eyes lit with amusement. Wendell had always known how to get a rise out of her.

"That's right, you have another birthday coming up in a few days, don't you, Em? What is it—thirty-nine? Forty?"

"It's thirty-*seven* and you damned well know it," she snapped, having located the correct page. "I'll see you after school." She hung up the phone to concentrate on the response to her scathing review.

"My dear Miss Jericho," Emily typed rapidly five minutes after she'd arrived home from school. Then, sighing in exasperation, she ripped the page from the typewriter and rolled in a fresh sheet. Miss Jericho was neither dear nor hers. Besides, it might not be Bonnie Jericho who'd written the insulting letter. Regional or not, there was no reason to think a best-selling author would bother to read a small-town daily, and there'd hardly been time for it to reach her through a clipping service.

A cool glint brightened Emily's normally grave eyes. "Dear B.J. Is that Betty Jane? Barbara Jo? Anonymous letters are both cowardly and abhorrent. I dignify yours with an answer only at the behest of my editor."

Which was not precisely true. All day long she'd been seething, to the point where she'd actually overlooked her students' inattentiveness and the stack of dog-eared romances that had exchanged hands during break. On the way out of the stifling room, she'd heard Kim Bleeker whispering, "Sandi, you've *got* to read this one and give it back tomorrow. Talk about every which way! Seven times, and once on *horseback!*"

She hadn't even bothered to light the fire before starting her reply to B.J. Could it be Jericho, after all? In spite of everything, Emily knew a momentary rush of excitement at the thought that she might actually be corresponding with the author of five best-sellers. And no matter how much she might despise the genre, she grudgingly admitted that for trash, they were well-written.

B.J. could be anyone. She could think of half-dozen people offhand whose initials fit, although she seriously doubted that Bob Jernigan at the service station would bother to write such a letter, and Barby Jarvis was only four years old. It was probably some frustrated, defensive romance reader. It might even be one of her own students, although the wording was a bit sophisticated for the average fifteen-year-old.

"Dear Betty Jane: I'm sorry you took exception to my review of *Reap the Wild Wind*. While I stand by my opinion, I will confess that my attitude is partially colored by the fact that Miss Jericho is obviously a skilled writer. It is unfortunate that she restricts herself to such unworthy subjects. Fairy tales of the type propounded by the so-called romance genre are an insult to the intellect of any thinking woman. They do our gender a disservice by raising expectations that can only lead to disillusionment, and are therefore to be despised."

She felt somewhat better after that. Lighting the fire she'd laid that morning, Emily sighed and slipped off her gray sling-back pumps. At times like this, with another birthday staring her in the face, she was apt to suffer from a mild sort of depression. Thirty-seven come Saturday, and what did she have to show for it? One engagement that had ended anticlimactically after two unexciting years, one career that grew less rewarding with every passing day, a part-time job that took too much of her time for the paltry rewards it brought, and a drafty house chock-full of furniture that was neither old enough to be valuable nor attractive enough to be desirable.

She had Libby and Vangie, the sisters she'd raised from ages ten and eleven respectively. She'd done her best with them, and all in all, they'd turned out to be people she liked as well as loved, but they were caught up in their own affairs now. Neither of them had wanted to come back to the Eastern Shore, where too many unhappy memories lingered. She couldn't blame them for that.

Thirty-seven. For the hundredth time she considered selling out, moving away and starting over. She was still young enough to do it. If lately she'd felt far older than her years, it was her own fault. She'd been so caught up in the treadmill of classroom and homework, of rushing through books just so she could grind out her reviews, of trying to fit in all the chores that went along with owning an elderly house, that she never took time for herself.

When was the last time she'd seen a movie? Or even walked in the woods? How long had it been since she'd found time to relax, to take an apple, a bit of cheese and a glass of wine to the shore, where she'd watch birds, or poke about the water's edge, examining pebbles and the occasional potsherd she found there? So the peninsula had changed hands—there were no fences to keep her out, no signs proclaiming the new ownership. Nothing had really changed.

As soon as the rain stopped, Emily promised herself resolutely, she'd put together a picnic and find a sunny spot near the water where she could lie back and watch the sails buffeting back and forth out on the bay. What was the point in owning a waterfront cottage if one didn't take time to appreciate it?

By Saturday the sky was a joyous shade of blue, with only an occasional wisp of lavender cloud to mark the passing cold front. There were a dozen chores to be done, and Emily delighted for once in ignoring them all.

Humming an unrecognizable version of the overture to *Der Rosenkavalier,* she ducked her head under the spray and lathered the abundance of glossy brown hair. Today was her birthday and she was determined to enjoy it. One day soon she'd treat herself to a new coat, since the cleaners had been unable to locate her old one. She didn't have to go overboard—a modest chinchilla should do it.

"Or a black mink?" she suggested to her image as she blotted the moisture from her hair. The steamy mirror was flattering, especially as her cheeks were still flushed from her bath. "As the woman in the TV ad says," she told herself, assuming a sultry pose, "I'm worth it."

Actually, she was holding up pretty well, all things

considered. She'd inherited the McClouds' spare frame—long, nicely shaped legs, narrow hands and feet. Her cheekbones were the sort that aged well, and her eyes were nice enough. Perhaps she'd start wearing more makeup—a little more eye shadow, a touch of blusher. Lately she'd got out of the habit.

The scent of woodsmoke tantalized her nostrils before she'd even left the yard. She'd always loved campfires and burning leaves, but if someone had dropped a cigarette in the woods and set fire to a patch of brush, that was another matter. If Bon-Bey's woods burned, then so did hers, and Bon-Bey, Inc. wasn't here to police their property.

Following the trail of the acrid smoke, Emily angled toward the far shore of the point, an area she seldom visited, as there were many more accessible places that were every bit as lovely. It was encouragingly damp once she entered the deepest woods, but along the shore there'd be patches of marsh grass and low shrubbery that would dry quickly in the sunlight.

She almost tripped over it. In the mellow gloom of an autumn forest, the last thing Emily expected to see was a motorcycle. A few feet away stood a small tent. Before she could react to those two items, she saw the man. Broad, red-clad shoulders tapered downward to narrow hips, revealing a band of tanned flesh between shirt and jeans. His back was to her as he hunched over a small fire.

Emily's heart leapt into double-time and she froze mid-stride. Her eyes took in the leather jacket flung across the motorcycle and the short-handled ax wedged in a fallen oak. There was no one around for a dozen miles—unless he was only one of a gang who was using the isolated place for . . . for whatever motorcycle gangs used isolated places like this for. She could scream her head off and no one would hear her.

Before she could break the momentary paralysis and edge away from the small clearing, the intruder stood and turned in a smooth motion that reminded her of a fox she'd once seen in these woods. There was something about his face—wary, but unafraid. She recognized him instantly. It was the same man who'd offered help outside the dry cleaners several days before. Had he followed her home? Was he planning to . . . ? But that was ridiculous! Not in broad daylight—not here in her own backyard!

They stood poised, neither of them speaking as the tiny fire crackled and sparked behind a circle of rocks. Emily, her brain working quite coolly now, evaluated her chances of escaping should he prove aggressive. They were of a height, but her legs might be longer. On the other hand, he had wheels. She didn't fancy being chased through the woods by an angry motorcyclist. He was obviously tough and fit and totally unafraid. He was also a trespasser, someone who had no business even being in these woods, much less camping here.

"Would you care for a chocolate-and-marshmallow graham cracker?" the trespasser inquired as politely as if he were in his own drawing room offering milk for her tea.

She'd been unconsciously holding her breath since that first involuntary gasp. Now the air rushed from her lungs. What sort of motorcyclist would offer her something like that? A member of Heck's Angels?

Emily subdued an unlikely urge to giggle.

"Smores?" she inquired, her husky contralto quivering in relief and amusement.

He blinked. Even from this distance she was aware of the intensity of his gaze. Tilting his head inquisitively, he smiled, and Emily felt something inside her shift, leaving an oddly hollow feeling in its place.

"The . . . the graham crackers with chocolate and marshmallow melted on them. When I was young, we called them smores. You know—some more?" She hadn't moved; they were still a dozen yards apart. She wondered if he'd heard the peculiar breathlessness in her voice. Swallowing nervously, she recalled something about wild creatures being able to smell fear in a human being.

God knows she'd been scared out of her wits for a minute there. And she wasn't out of the woods yet—either figuratively or literally.

"I've got a pot of water all ready for coffee. Even with the sun out, it's cold back here in the woods." Bey waited for her to advance or retreat. He'd heard her approach even before she'd caught her breath—a split second before. There'd been times in his life when a split second's warning had been all that had saved his skin.

Silk and handmade lace and hundred-dollar-an-ounce perfume, he'd summed her up instantly. Even in gray wool slacks covered in beggar's-lice and a suede jacket that was shiny at the cuffs and collar, she was a class act. She was the sort of woman who seldom came his way. He'd thought about her once or twice since he'd seen her grinding away at that old clunker she drove. A woman like that should be driving a Mercedes, at least. Better yet, she should be chauffeured.

The half-grin thawed into a genuine smile. "Come hunker down at the fire. I've got a spare cup here somewhere."

Stiffly Emily began to move, feeling strangely as if she were a puppet and someone else was pulling the strings. She wasn't accustomed to "hunkering down" to anything—especially not with a barbarian who rode a motorcycle and wore muddy jeans with what looked suspiciously like the top of a set of long johns. She halted several yards away. "These woods are posted, you know," she said evenly.

"I'm not hurting anything." Bey watched her eyes, his subliminal senses taking in the easy way she moved. He liked tall women. This one carried herself as proudly as a clipper ship.

Emily found herself engaged in an unexpectedly intimate examination of the man, of his muscular, compact build, his irregular features, the deceptively relaxed way he held himself, like a coiled spring ready to fire off at a touch. He was a sort she'd seldom encountered personally. "There are signs up all along the boundary warning trespassers away," she pointed out.

Hazel eyes captured gray ones easily, holding them prisoner for long, uncomfortable moments. "I have permission to be here," Bey said quietly, perversely refusing to release her gaze. She had strength and pride. He admired that in a woman.

"From whom?" Emily demanded breathlessly, breaking away finally from his disconcerting spell. If this man even knew who owned the property, it would surprise her. He had to be bluffing.

"Let's just say the new owner knows I'm here. More

to the point, who are you, and what's your business here?"

Feeling suddenly weak, Emily dropped down onto the dead oak, digging her fingers into the punky wood. She could pretend that she still owned the whole tract—it would lend her more authority. But there was always the off-chance that he was telling the truth. "Did you say coffee?" she blurted more from confusion than from thirst. If it wasn't outright surrender, it was close to it. At least the man had the courtesy not to gloat.

"Hope you don't take anything in yours." He turned away, busying himself at the fireside for a moment before returning to hand her a steaming, battered mug. She took both sugar and cream, actually, but she was on thin ice here—best to be diplomatic until she could politely take her leave.

He joined her on the log, cupping his strong, surprisingly well-kept hands around an even more battered mug. "In a minute I'll make us some . . . What did you call 'em? Smores? I thought they were my own invention."

Emily sipped cautiously at the scalding brew, amazed at finding herself here in the middle of the woods calmly sharing black coffee with a man who could be a member of an infamous motorcycle gang, for all she knew. "Hmmm, instant," she remarked, immediately regretting her tactlessness.

"You don't drink instant coffee?"

"It's fine, it's just perfect," she lied hastily.

"At least you've got no grounds for complaint."

Emily shot him a quick glance. At the sight of wickedly gleaming eyes in a suspiciously solemn face,

41

she felt the edge of her reserve begin to crumble. "That's abominable," she accused with a straight face.

"I know. Don't you like abominable jokes either?"

"About as much as I like instant coffee. What did you measure it with, a shovel?"

"A knife blade, as a matter of fact. Three bladefuls per cup."

"Try one," Emily suggested dryly, sipping the bitter beverage cautiously.

Without speaking, he took her mug, poured out a third of the coffee and refilled the cup with water from the smoke-blackened pot. He watched as she tried it again. "Better?" he asked solicitously.

Emily considered a courteous lie and decided against it. She had an idea this man would see through any such polite fabrication. Besides, what did it matter? "It's still terrible, but if you like it this way, that's your privilege."

"You live around here?" the man asked genially. He had a surprisingly nice voice—deep, soft, with an accent that was impossible to pin down.

She nodded, caution preventing her from revealing the details. "I used to walk here a lot. It's one of the few places I know where you can't hear the traffic noises."

"I noticed. Many people find their way out here?" The question was casually put, but Emily had the feeling that her answer was of more than casual interest.

"All the time," she prevaricated. "Hunters, fishermen, bird watchers, scout troups. There's a botany class scheduled to be here any minute now—oh, and I forgot the joggers."

He shot her a skeptical look. "What about the house at the edge of the woods? The one with the green door and shutters?"

Emily leaned over and picked up a purplish sweet-gum leaf, twirling it between her fingers as she considered a reply. "What about it?"

"Would that be your house?" It was a shot in the dark, but he knew with a growing certainty that this woman was the elderly party he'd been trying to contact off and on for several weeks.

Emily nodded. It would do little good to deny it—anyone in town could tell him as much if he were really interested. At least he didn't know she lived alone. And even if he did, there was something about him that, oddly enough, she instinctively trusted. For all his toughness, there was a directness about him that appealed to her.

"My name's Bey Jones. That's Bey with an E, not an A. What's yours?"

Well, that was direct enough. "Emily McCloud," she replied, digging up a half-buried pine cone with the toe of her suede moccasin.

For a minute she thought he hadn't heard her. And then he turned and extended a hand. "Miss McCloud," he acknowledged softly, his smile just as wide, but somehow different. "I'm your new neighbor."

She'd left him soon after that. Thrown off balance by a subtle change that followed the introduction, Emily had made the excuse of something in the oven and hurried away. Later she wished she'd taken the time to ask a few pertinent questions. Such as what he planned to do with the property. And exactly who he was, and where he was from, and what he did, and if there was a Mrs. Bey Jones.

Bey with an E. Then it hadn't been a typo. She'd been upset at having to sell the property and a misspelled word had been the least of her worries. She was so accustomed to seeing the word "bay" on so many businesses around the Eastern Shore that she hadn't even thought about it.

Bon-Bey was his corporation, then. What sort of corporation? Surely the place hadn't been rezoned; she'd have been notified if that had been the case. A residence? A development?

Oh Lord, not a housing development! Bon-Bey was a real-estate outfit, then—she'd bet her bottom dollar on it. The way her luck had been running just recently, it had to be that.

If she'd needed a shove to boost her out of a rut, this was it. What a birthday present! A card from Libby, a scarf from Vangie, and a tract of cracker-box houses going up right under her nose.

On Sunday morning, she drove into Baltimore. She'd always found aquariums soothing, and the National Aquarium was precisely what she needed at the moment. And after she'd sorted herself out, she'd treat herself to an expensive lunch and a new winter coat. That done, she'd consider the facts calmly and decide whether or not to put her house on the market and hand in her notice at school. If the school didn't hand its notice to her first.

Staring unseeingly at the glass wall as a white shark passed within three inches of her nose, Emily sighed again. At this rate, she'd soon be hyperventilated. She'd been sighing all weekend.

The perfectly idiotic thing was, she couldn't get Bey Jones out of her mind. The academy was facing bankruptcy, her salary had been drastically cut, there was no chance of making up the difference with another column. She was now officially thirty-seven years old and facing a housing development right on her doorstep, and all she could think about was a tough-looking man who rode a motorcycle and camped in the woods and made atrocious coffee.

A man, her relentless thoughts added, who had a crooked smile and a way of laughing with his eyes that made a battered face seem amazingly desirable.

The trucks came before she even left the house on Monday morning. Three pickup trucks followed by a behemoth with a gaping steel jaw. Emily stood on her front porch, briefcase and purse hanging limply from one hand, and watched the ominous parade.

It had started then—the ruthless bulldozing, the crushing of everything precious and lovely in her woods—the woods where she'd picnicked with her grandfather as a child, a consolation for having all her parents' attention claimed by the two babies.

As though sensing that something was seriously wrong, her girls were unusually subdued all day. When Denise Boger actually claimed Conrad Aiken's obscure *Samadha* as her favorite poem of the term, Emily could have wept.

"It's sort of like the way it is now, Miss McCloud. We've got these trees out behind the swimming pool, and every fall they sort of like . . . well, the pool gets all full of leaves, and the trees shine down in it, and . . . well, you know."

Perhaps she was doing them a disservice to foster

sensitivity and an appreciation for beauty, Emily thought despairingly. By the time they were her age, all the beauty might have been bulldozed off the face of the earth. Sensitivity could be a handicap.

By the time she dropped off her copy and collected another stack of books, Emily had herself in hand again. She collected the mail, dropped it along with her purse and briefcase on the Biedermeier sofa—it made a wonderful table—and lighted the fire. By the time she'd changed into gray slacks and a violet cashmere pullover Libby had left behind, she was completely composed.

Next year she'd indulge herself in another maudlin bout of self-searching. One a year was all she could afford. Time brought changes; it was inevitable. It didn't pay to look back at what might have been, or worry too much about what was to come. Sufficient unto the day . . .

The peremptory rap on the door came while she was setting a single Wedgwood plate on the table with one hand and stirring the Stroganoff with the other. Muttering an impatient "I'm coming" under her breath, she hurried through the living room, dodging nimbly around the bulky pump organ and swinging her hips to avoid the projecting arm of a rather ugly Morris chair.

"Bey?" she said in some confusion at the sight of her visitor.

"Miss McCloud," he repeated. He was wearing the same shirt and the same jeans, as far as she could tell. With one muscular arm braced against the doorjamb, he looked perfectly relaxed.

Her confusion increased at his formal greeting. "Mr. Jones?" she said uncertainly. She'd somehow thought that first names were in order after the few minutes of camaraderie they'd shared.

"I saw your light," he murmured, his eyes never leaving hers.

Disconcerted at his nearness—they'd been several feet apart on the oak log in the woods—she stepped back and issued a hesitant invitation. "Won't you . . . come in?"

She could feel the animal warmth of him as he brushed past her. His scent, a mixture of woodsmoke and some excitingly masculine essence, assailed her nostrils and threatened to rob her of her newly regained composure. She stood there staring helplessly at his back while he turned slowly to examine her room.

He was little taller than she was, and yet his presence seemed to push out the walls and lift the ceiling. There was a force about the man that was somehow larger than life. It frightened her, and she wanted him out—out of her house, out of her life.

"Did you . . . were you . . . ?" she stammered, hardly knowing what to say without sounding rude.

"I stayed over another couple of days since the weather's clear. Had to go into town and stock up on provisions."

"Oh," she said lamely. And then, lifting her head at the smell from the kitchen, she blurted, "Excuse me, will you? Something's burning."

Not quite, but almost. The sour cream, wine and mushroom sauce was dried around the edges of the pan.

"Were you in time?" Bey asked. He watched her stirring the mixture, agitating the narrow strips of beef, her lips pursed in annoyance.

He'd intended to stay away—he'd managed to put her out of his mind for two whole days, but as he'd passed her house a few minutes ago, his curiosity had risen up stronger than ever. How could a woman as beautiful and as obviously intelligent as Emily McCloud write such a narrow-minded, vindictive review of what was a damned fine book, if he did say so himself? He was no longer furious with her—he was merely curious.

In the moment before she turned to answer him, his gaze lingered appreciatively on the subtle curve of her lean hips. There was a special allure in subtlety. He'd appreciated plenty of voluptuous women in his rambling years, but there was something about this particular woman that set her apart.

"It wasn't quite scorched," Emily admitted, switching off the burner and lifting the lid to stir the pot of rice. It was ready—the table was set. "I suppose you've had dinner," she murmured, avoiding those compelling hazel eyes. "I'm running late tonight."

"Guess I am, too," Bey replied equably, taking in the single plate, the sparkling wineglass, the crisp linen napkin and the heavy, ornate silver. "It won't take me long to get a fire going, though. Once it burns down, I'll have the can all opened and ready to heat."

Emily closed her eyes momentarily and wondered if he was doing it deliberately. "You're welcome to share my dinner," she heard herself offer.

Bey levered himself away from the doorway where he'd been leaning, arms crossed over his chest. "I wasn't hinting, Miss McCloud."

Irritably Emily reached for another plate. "I wasn't implying that you were, Mr. Jones."

"Oh, well, in that case, I thank you." He was beside

her without seeming to have moved, taking the silverware from her hand and placing it on the table beside the second plate. Dense bronze lashes shielding his eyes, he arranged the utensils with perfect precision and accepted the linen napkin with a nod of thanks.

Emily could have kicked herself. He was acting like a wistful little boy, and she knew damned well there wasn't a boyish bone in his body. Bey Jones was tough as nails. She must have been insane to invite him into her home.

"I hope you like Stroganoff," she grumbled, not caring if she sounded ungracious.

3

·❦❦❦❦❦❦❦❦❦❦·

Sure do," Bey replied, a crooked grin simmering across his irregular features. "Shall I pour the wine for you?"

"It's in the refrigerator." Emily reached for another of her Grandmother Barrington's hand-etched lead-crystal wineglasses. "Or perhaps you'd prefer coffee?" she added, glancing over her shoulder with a suspiciously grave expression.

At Bey's look of swift comprehension, her gravity dissolved into a smile that lingered as she took down another bowl and began dividing the salad.

"Hey, if that's for me, don't bother." Bey uncorked the wine and steadied the glass as he poured, his sinewy hands incongruous on the fragile stem.

"You don't care for any salad?" Emily's eyes shifted from his face to his hands and back again, her senses suddenly jolted by the sight of so much concentrated masculinity against the familiar background of her breakfast nook.

"I can live without it."

"I'm afraid I don't have another vegetable."

"You have rice," Bey replied agreeably.

"Rice is not a vegetable."

"Sure it is, I've seen it growing." Bey pulled out her chair, his arms spreading in a half-embrace as he seated her at the table.

"It's a grain," Emily pointed out as she served his plate with a generous mound of brown rice and ladled on a lion's share of the richly sauced beef.

"A technicality," Bey rejoined calmly. He spread the napkin across his thighs and grimaced apologetically. "I'm not exactly dressed for dining out."

She shrugged. "Neither am I."

"You're in. I'm the one who's out." Fork poised, he studied the woman across from him. He hadn't paid much attention to what she had on—she was the sort of woman who made clothes seem irrelevant. Whatever she was wearing was the right thing to wear. An errant thought brought a speculative gleam to his eyes and he quickly lowered them to his plate.

"This is good," he said a few moments later, offering her one of those hazardous smiles of his that threatened to undermine every shred of her hard-earned equilibrium. "Living outdoors is a real appetizer."

That said, he devoted himself to cleaning off his plate, the task of a few moments. Emily wondered guiltily if she should have given him all the Stroganoff and settled for the spinach-and-mushroom salad as her share. He had a sort of coiled-spring vitality that indicated a voracious appetite.

The plain truth was, he rattled her. It had been bad enough in the open woods, but here in the intimacy of her own small home, it was far worse. There was no place in her settled life-style for a man like Bey Jones.

She'd be polite, but cool, she decided firmly. She'd get rid of the man as soon as she possibly could without being actually discourteous.

"Do you live in this area, Mr. Jones?"

"I'm working on it, and make it Bey, will you . . . Emily? That's a nice name. Are there many Emily McClouds around these parts? I seem to recall the realtor's saying you come from an old Eastern Shore family."

"I have a sister in California and another in Paris, both married. As far as I know, I'm the only McCloud left. I didn't make dessert, Bey. Would you care for coffee?" Above a carefully controlled mouth, Emily's eyes sparkled unexpectedly. "I'm afraid I can't offer you anything but the drip variety."

"I'd like that—in front of your fireplace?" Bey asked hopefully. "I'm going to have a fireplace before this winter's done. Here, let me help you with those dishes."

Rising hastily, Emily reached a protective hand toward the fragile crystal. She regretted it even before she saw the quick flare of his nostrils. She didn't have to insult the man by implication. "I . . . I'll just leave them for later," she murmured apologetically. "Would you see if the fire needs tending while I start the coffee?"

He shrugged, the collarless red knit shirt following

the smooth play of muscles that produced the expressive gesture. Wordlessly he sauntered into the living room, leaving Emily both angry and bewildered.

What *was* there about this man that affected her so strongly? He certainly wasn't the sort of man she usually invited into her home, but since she had, it was rude, not to mention unfair, to imply that he was a barbarian who couldn't be trusted in polite society.

She knew absolutely nothing about him—for all she knew, he could be lying about everything. In the short time since she'd first laid eyes on him, he'd managed to invade her consciousness in a way that no man had done in years. Irritably she dismissed the thought that perhaps it was herself she didn't trust.

The coffee poured, she handed Bey a cup and nodded to the cushioned Morris chair. Then, gracefully balancing her own cup and saucer in one long, slender hand, she lowered herself onto the inhospitable sofa. "I saw the trucks and that monstrous-looking digging thing go by this morning."

"The backhoe?" Bracing his shoulders against the chintz cushion, Bey stretched out his legs and crossed his booted ankles.

Emily wished rather desperately that he'd either get himself a looser pair of jeans or sit in a more circumspect manner—so much potent masculinity at close range was disconcerting. It had been too long since she'd entertained anyone more exciting than the local minister; she simply wasn't prepared for a man who flaunted his sexuality without even being aware of it.

"A backhoe," she repeated, forcing her mind into a safer channel. "That's sort of like a bulldozer, isn't it? Bey, I do hope you plan to leave a few trees standing." Small hope; a cycle-riding ruffian who wore undershirts, tight jeans and resoled boots would probably timber the place and then resell it for farmland.

Bey, cradling the delicate violet-sprigged cup in his square, tanned hands, glanced slowly about the room, making no effort to reassure her. Unless he were a junk dealer, Emily thought rancorously, no man could be all that interested in her accumulation of mismatched furniture.

For a long moment his gaze rested on an untidy stack of papers on the breakfront. He shifted his weight, and in silent desperation she watched the play of muscles under the faded denim. Then, tearing her eyes away from his powerful thighs, she studied his face in an effort to probe his mind. The man was not quite so simple as she'd first imagined. Oh, she'd soon recognized the little-boy-lost game he was playing—it had probably got him into more than a few kitchens. More than a few beds, as well.

But there was another game being played here. She sensed it without understanding it, and it made her uneasy. "What exactly are you planning to build, Bey?"

His gaze wandered back to move over her face with the same degree of detachment he'd shown the pump organ, the striped sofa, the imperfect breakfront and the assortment of mismatched chairs. Slightly less, she noted in dismay, than he'd shown her overflowing bookshelves.

"Just a home," he said. "You know—fireplace, kitchen, lots of windows. You're invited to trespass anytime you feel like it." The detachment shifted and his expression warmed—a trick done with mirrors, Emily decided.

"Thanks," she said dryly, "but I'm afraid the woods have lost a great deal of their appeal."

His smile grew infectious, creasing his weathered cheeks into what might have been considered dimples in a lesser man. "I promise you, I'm not taking down a single tree unnecessarily—just enough to squeeze in one small house. You'll never even know it's there."

She'd know, all right. She was going to have to be on her guard every minute until she'd figured out exactly why Bey Jones affected her the way he did. It wasn't reasonable. It wasn't even rational! "For you and your family?" she hazarded.

"For me. I'm not married."

"Oh, well, I didn't . . . I mean, it's of no concern to me . . ." She broke off. Listen to her! He was doing it to her again! Looking at her that way, as if she were some intriguing botanical specimen he'd come across unexpectedly. The next thing she knew, he'd be pulling her petals off.

She tugged at the neck of her sweater. She'd asked him to tend the fire, and he'd thrown on more logs. At this rate she'd have to order another cord of wood before Thanksgiving.

"Did I overdo it?" Bey asked apologetically. "Sorry —I've got a thing about fireplaces. Love 'em. Never had one."

She edged as far away from the blaze as she could, but in a room the size of her small living room, there was nowhere to go. "Maybe I should open the front door," she muttered in desperation.

"Better yet, why don't we take a walk, watch the moon come up over the bay. By the time we get back, the fire will have burned down some."

She had to do something—she was sweltering.

Perspiration bloomed on her back, making the sweater itch abominably. With no makeup to disguise it, her face was probably beet red. "Well . . . maybe just a short walk," she conceded. "I have some work to get done before tomorrow."

"I don't think you mentioned what you did, Emily."

"Neither did you," Emily retorted.

"I asked you first." He was standing so close she could see the shadow of golden stubble against his tanned skin. Suddenly she felt an overwhelming compulsion to touch him. "I teach English at a girls' school," she blurted.

He nodded thoughtfully. "Better wear a coat, you're soaking wet."

Emily got out her suede jacket and he took it from her hands, holding it while she ran her arms into the sleeves. The touch of his hands on her neck as he settled it into place brought still more heat to her face.

I'm having a mid-life crisis, she thought wildly. *That sort of thing is supposed to be mental rather than physical, but heaven help me, this is both!*

There was just enough light from the stars to make out the yellow clay road. "This way," she murmured, curling her hands into her pocket and hurrying across the rutted road to an overgrown path that led down to the water. Halfway down, she halted, and Bey cannoned into her back.

"Ouch! I think I'm caught." Cautiously she felt for the briar that had snagged her slacks.

His hands covered hers in the darkness. "Don't move—let me help you." His voice was as soft as the silver seedheads that swayed heavily on the nearby reeds—soft, with a kernel of hardness at the center.

She couldn't move; clawlike thorns were digging into her thigh. As uncomfortable as she was, Bey's fingers moving carefully over her leg through a layer of thin wool gabardine made matters still worse. Her hair, which she usually wore anchored in a tidy knot, was coming down, and she shoved at it ineffectually.

"I don't feel it anymore," she murmured finally, easing away from the grip of a warm hand just above her knee.

"Think I got 'em all." He was closer than she'd expected, and when he stood, his words brushed warmly past her ear.

"Look, this wasn't such a good idea," Emily protested weakly. "I can't see a darned thing and the moon probably won't be up for hours."

"O ye of little faith. See that glow over there? What do you think that is?"

"That's the stadium at Easton," she said dryly. "They're having a night game."

Draping an arm across her shoulders, Bey swept her down the sloping path to the narrow strip of beach. "I always was a sucker for the romantic glow of stadium lights." Halting at the edge of the water, he whispered, "Look, there's a sloop coming in from the bay under sail—see her?"

Pointing with one hand, he leaned his face close to hers, and Emily felt her breath catch and hang somewhere in her throat.

"I don't see a thing," she managed, her voice barely audible. Furtively she wriggled away from the warm presence at her side.

"Don't look directly at what you're trying to see— look just above it and wait," Bey instructed softly.

"How can I tell where just above it is if I can't see it?" Her chattering words emerged on tiny clouds of vapor, and she drew in a sharp breath, savoring the musky scent of woodsmoke and soap and something devastatingly masculine. She was acutely aware of the contrast of the cold night air and the radiant warmth of his body; the space between them might just as well not be there for all the good it did her frayed nerves.

"I . . . I expect the fire's burned down by now," she said huskily.

"How long do you think we've been out here?" Laughter simmered under the dark surface of his voice.

"Half an hour?" The words were a hopeful plea.

Bey laughed aloud. His arm tightened briefly around her shoulders, and then he moved away. "Five minutes at most."

Emily continued to stare out over the dark water where the pale shape of a large sloop was beginning to emerge. Wrapping her arms about her chest, she shivered. "That's long enough. Let's go back." Torn by a strange reluctance to end the brief closeness and an overpowering need to escape, she turned and started up the bank.

Bey didn't offer to help her. From behind and below, he could see her slender, swaying back quite clearly. The feel of her was still on his hands. Eyes narrowing, he inhaled deeply. Was it only his heightened imagination, or could he still catch a hint of her clean floral scent mingling with the smell of mud and water and dried weeds?

His night vision was excellent; he followed her easily, admiring the sheer grace of her stride as she picked her way through the encroaching weeds. As he moved silently up the narrow path, it occurred to him that she was nervous as a cat.

A schoolteacher, hmmm? That might explain a certain academic bias, but there was more to it than that. She had style, beauty, wit and intelligence, and she was as nervous around him as a convent-reared virgin on her first date. What had turned her against men, soured her on romance? A bad affair? A failed marriage? Possibly. Whatever it was, it had hit her hard. She'd built up a lot of scar tissue.

He was still watching her when she reached the top of the bank. In a gesture of uncertainty that he filed away in his writer's mind for future use, she half-turned, shook her head and continued across the road without waiting.

Bey picked up his pace. Damned if she was going to barricade herself inside that stuffy little museum of hers—at least not until he had a few more answers. He had her where he wanted her now. She'd been dying of curiosity to know what he was going to do with Fletcher's Landing. It meant something to her, that tract of land—probably been in the family for generations. The McClouds were Old Family, landed gentry.

Gentry, maybe, but the land was now his. He'd paid twice what it was worth just to be sure he got it. He might not have much of a pedigree, but a hundred and twenty-two acres on the Chesapeake Bay was a pretty damned good consolation.

"Emily? Slow up," he called out softly.

At the edge of the uneven brick walk that led to her porch, Emily paused. Courtesy was too ingrained to allow her to dash inside and bar the door without a word. Striving for just the right note of chilly regret, she said, "I expect you have things to do, Bey—provisions to unpack and . . ." Her composure began to crumble. ". . . and, well . . . it's been a lovely evening, Bey."

He roared. His laughter assaulted Emily's newly vulnerable sensibilities, and she swung around and stalked up the shallow steps to her front door.

"Emily, wait—honey, I'm sorry." He took the two steps in a silent leap. Moving swiftly, he caught her at the door.

She tried to ignore him. Her hair was falling in ruins about her shoulders, and her teeth were clenched tightly to keep them from chattering. When a suspicion of a chuckle reached her, it was too much. She lifted her chin and turned, ready to shrivel him with a word, a look.

He was too close. The clean woodsy-musky scent of him, the animal warmth of his body, began leaching the strength from her bones. Their eyes were almost on a level.

"You seem to find me amusing, Mr. Jones. I was merely being courteous, you know. It was *not* a lovely evening." She gathered her courage and rushed on, her voice quivering from sheer nerves. "You barge into my house and devour my dinner—you turn my living room into a blast furnace, and you seem to think it's all some sort of a joke. I'm afraid I can't share your amusement, Mr. Jones."

Light from the door she'd left ajar spilled out to halo Bey's thick blond hair. His face was partly in shadow, but she could easily make out the dancing light in those hazel eyes, the gleam of his strong white teeth.

She could even see the tiny shadow where one of the front ones lapped slightly over its neighbor. Her hands clenched impotently at her sides. Damn the man, even his *teeth* were disarming!

Taking a deep, steadying breath, she said firmly, "I . . . I . . . good night!"

And still she stood there, her body stone deaf to the conflicting demands of her brain.

"Aren't you going to invite me in for a nightcap?"

Freshly affronted, she drew in a sharp breath. "Don't be absurd."

The white gleam of his grin widened. "Am I being absurd, Emily? Why are you so upset? You invited me to share your dinner, and as for the fire—I told you, I've never had a fireplace. How was I to know—?"

"Oh, forget it. I can always turn on the air conditioner."

"Don't bother. The temperature will drop several degrees the minute you set foot in the room. There's not a whole lot of warmth in you, is there, Emily McCloud?"

She fumbled for the knob behind her, unreasonably stung by his words. She'd heard them from Wendell more than once, and it hadn't bothered her all that much until now.

Before she could slide through the door, Bey's hands moved to capture her arms. He was incredibly strong, but she was no weakling. "I don't appreciate being mauled, Bey," she said bitingly, twisting stiffly against the relentless grip of his fingers.

"I could never back down from a challenge."

"I am *not* a challenge," she seethed, turning her face away from the compelling intensity of his eyes.

"And I refuse to engage in a brawl. If you're going to . . . to kiss me, then do it and get it over with."

She heard the sharp intake of his breath. For an instant his fingers bit into her arms painfully. Tears of frustration filmed her eyes and she blinked them away. How on earth had she got herself into such a degrading situation, engaging in a wrestling match on her front porch as if she were no more mature than one of her own students.

Slowly he released her, his hands trailing off her arms to hook into his belt. He stepped back, and momentarily paralyzed, Emily was unable to escape his scathing words.

"Lady, I've picked up a few scars in my lifetime," Bey grated softly, his merciless eyes cutting through every layer of protection she'd acquired over the years, "but so far I've managed to avoid being frostbitten. If it's all the same to you, I think I'll pass up your offer."

Emily closed the door and leaned against it, eyes closed, fists pressing against her thighs. Damn, damn, *damn!* She'd never been so humiliated. Not even when she'd had to ask Wendell for a raise. Not even when she'd failed her first driver's exam three times for the same stupid mistake, with half her high-school class looking on.

Neighbors or not, she'd have nothing more to do with him. It shouldn't be all that difficult. People in big cities lived next door to each other for years without meeting. She had no reason to go into the woods, and Bey certainly wouldn't be turning up on her doorstep again. Whatever he'd been looking for, he hadn't found it here; he'd certainly made that plain enough.

Bey sat on a bench, notebook in hand, and glared at the woman he'd been observing so carefully for almost forty-five minutes. She was his third try today; he'd wasted an entire morning. He'd picked up her trail down by the ship the *Constellation* and managed to keep her in sight, meanwhile making notes on the way she moved and the way her hair slithered over her shoulders when she turned her head to speak to the man beside her. He'd tried out his heroine's name on her—Belinda. Not a perfect fit, but . . . possible.

He already knew Belinda's perfume, her favorite wine, the authors she read and the music she liked most. Somehow, this woman looked more like a cocktail type, but never mind. She probably preferred rock over Rachmaninoff, too, and never read anything heavier than a fashion magazine, but his imagination could span the gap. The buzz words he'd jotted down were "elegant," "well-bred," "modest," "spirited."

And then she'd paused not three feet away from where he loitered, pretending to take notes on various yachts anchored in the harbor. Scowling, she'd lifted a small, shapely foot, bringing with it a trail of stringy pink gum. Focusing wide, limpid eyes—nearsighted, he suspected—on her companion, she'd let fly a string of oaths that would have singed the hair off a drill sergeant's chest.

Bey ripped out the page of notes and crumpled it in one fist. That cut it! Dammit, at this rate he'd never find his heroine! He'd been coming down here to the inner harbor every day this week, looking for the personification of his female character. He'd long since discovered that it made his work immensely easier if he could find a woman who fit the mental image of his current heroine and watch her move about, hear her speak.

The outline had been going so well. He'd had it more or less roughed out in his head before he'd come back to Baltimore, but the minute he'd started fleshing out his protagonists, he'd found himself in trouble. His male character was no problem; it was Belinda who refused to solidify. She'd been waiting quietly in the back of his mind ever since he'd conceived the plot line, but then somehow, as soon as he'd started bringing it together, she'd started falling apart. Blond hair had given way to brown, green eyes to gray, and a beguiling little vest-pocket Venus had grown into a tall, willowy woman who walked as proudly as if there were five miles of red carpet unrolling before her feet.

All right, so be it. He wasn't locked into any particular physical type, but dammit, he had to make her come alive! This morning, in disgust, he'd covered the typewriter and gone hunting; he'd followed three women, none of whom had been quite right. Wasn't there a woman anywhere these days who fit his requirements? Either they dressed like hookers or frumps, or they moved like water buffalo, or they opened their mouths and spewed out sewage.

He raked a hand through his wildly untidy hair as a gust of cold, damp wind bit through his fatigue jacket. Maybe he was looking in the wrong place, but he'd tried hanging around some of the better shops inside. He'd moved out here when he'd begun to attract the interest of the security guards.

It was a simple enough quest: brown hair, gray

eyes, fairly tall, good bone structure. So why had every brown-haired, gray-eyed woman in Baltimore suddenly chosen to stay holed up all week?

Ramming the battered spiral notebook in his hip pocket, Bey took the steps, dodging browsers as he cut through the shopping mall. He crossed the street against the light and retrieved the BMW from the parking lot.

Dammit, he might as well have gone to the Landing this weekend for all he'd accomplished. He'd planned to have a chapter roughed out and the opening scene of another one by now.

After giving her black silk suit a last-minute once-over, Emily touched her hair, pressed her glossy lips together, and switched out the bedroom light. There was absolutely no reason why she shouldn't go out to dinner with an old friend. Lord knows, Wendell was no threat to her heart, nor she to his; it was simply a matter of survival. She'd been letting herself get into a rut. How long had it been since she'd gone out to dinner, much less dancing? Of course, it would have been nice if Wendell had done the asking, but she'd been too desperate to stand on ceremony.

Punctual as always, Wendell drove up just as she was draping her new gray chesterfield around her shoulders. After checking the latch, she hurried out and slid into the front seat.

"What made you change your mind, if you'll pardon my curiosity?" he asked as he backed around and headed toward town.

"It just occurred to me that I was getting stale. I felt like getting out, meeting new people."

"You do know how to flatter a man, don't you?"

"Did you want me to lie to you?"

"Heaven forbid," he said dryly. "You were always a stickler for truth and duty, weren't you?"

"How did duty get into this?" Emily relaxed into the heady comfort of Wendell's luxury sedan. "Is this thing new? I must say, I'm impressed."

"Are you? Tell me, Em, do you ever regret it?"

In the soft light from the instruments, she studied his lean profile, the long aquiline nose, the softening jawline. Did she regret it? After a comfortable silence that extended for several miles, she said, "It wouldn't have worked, Wendell. We're too much alike. I never realized that before, did you?"

"Mmmhmm. I've always known it. That's precisely why we didn't make it. You were honor-bound to take on the girls and all the responsibility that entailed, and I was honor-bound to take on the *Light* and all its encumbrances and liabilities. I suppose we had no choice. Neither one of us could offer the single-mindedness each of us needed in a mate."

Wendell lighted a cigarette and switched on the radio to a new station. Emily, unconsciously stroking the raw silk of her skirt, stared at the approaching lights of St. Michaels and considered his words.

So where did that leave her now that her responsibility to the girls was all but finished? With a house that was sadly in need of repairs, a career that was growing shakier by the day, one that had never brought her the satisfaction she'd hoped for. Her friends were all married, most of them living elsewhere, and she was so busy trying to make ends meet she hadn't had time even to keep up with her hobby. Her paints were all dried up, her brushes probably moth-eaten by now.

And just lately, there'd been a new feeling of restlessness, a sense of something vital that was lacking in her life. She didn't even know what it was, much less how to go about finding it.

4

Another letter to the editor. Emily had hoped the matter would die a quiet death. She was sorry now she'd ever read *Reap the Wild Wind,* much less written that review. Still, seeing the way her girls pored over such books, what choice had she had? These so-called romances that were cropping up everywhere today were insidiously believable. Judging by their popularity, there were hundreds of thousands of poor women being set up for the inevitable fall.

Scowling, she folded the newspaper into quarters and propped it against the coffeepot while she buttered her toast. This thing had gone far enough, regardless of what Wendell said. Her eyes scanned the page quickly and snagged on the initials B.J. The letter above the ambiguous abbreviated signature was short and to the point.

"Your reviewer admits that Miss Jericho's novel was well-written. One can only assume that it's the subject matter she finds so offensive. Would Miss McCloud have us clear our shelves of Jane Austen and the Brownings, of Dumas, Shakespeare and the Brontës? What do you have against love, Miss McCloud?"

Emily groaned, her anger increasing as she read the next few lines. This thing was getting completely out of hand. How could a simple book review have evolved into a public wrangle concerning her personal life? She could well imagine how everyone at the paper was taking this. They all knew she'd once been engaged to Wendell. By now they probably thought she'd been unilaterally dumped by their managing editor and was still nursing a broken heart.

"One more letter and that's *it*," she vowed, mentally composing a stinging reply that would put an end to the whole ridiculous affair.

By Friday afternoon Emily was more than ready for a break. One of her seniors had come in sporting an engaged-to-be-engaged ring, and it had proved of far greater interest than the early-twentieth-century poets. Her head was throbbing, and it was all she could do to give out the weekend assignment.

"Read Rupert Brooke's war poems in chapter three, and on Monday we'll compare them to his prewar work. That's all, girls," she finished, lifting her voice above the noisy exodus.

The last student darted out just as the headmistress came in. "You're getting famous, Emily," Abbie declared, tossing a copy of the *Light* on Emily's desk.

"Oh, no, not again," Emily wailed. She slipped a

sheaf of unfinished reports into her briefcase and reached for the morning paper. What did it take to put an end to this stupid duel?

"You mean you haven't seen it yet?"

Rustling the pages, Emily shook her head. "Didn't have time. Car wouldn't start and I had to call Bob to come out and jump the battery."

"I wonder if B.J. really is Bonnie Jericho," the straw-thin redhead murmured, leaning over to reread the latest letter on the editorial page. " 'The lady doth protest too much, methinks.' " She ran a nicotine-stained forefinger down the page. "Knows her *Hamlet,* anyway."

"Right now," Emily seethed, "the only *Hamlet* I can think of is 'murder most foul.' Where does she get off, telling everyone that I've obviously allowed my personal deprivations to color my intellectual judgment? That was a perfectly objective review, dammit! If you ask me, our friend B.J. sounds suspiciously defensive. She's obviously showing off with the *Hamlet,* trying to make me think she's not just a romance junkie."

"Don't underestimate us romance readers, Em— we're not exactly cases of arrested development, you know."

"Did I hit a nerve?" Emily inquired dryly. "Just how many a week do you account for?"

"About six, if I'm lucky. Want to borrow some? I just finished a really knockout book about this woman lawyer who's defending—"

"Abbie, don't *do* this to me," Emily sighed, shouldering her heavy purse and collecting her stuffed briefcase. Another weekend of work. She'd be lucky if she got through this mess by Monday.

"You try too hard, Em. No woman could possibly be as immune to romance as you pretend to be."

"Who's pretending?" Emily denied irritably. "I just can't see wasting so much time reading fairy tales."

"When's the last time you read one?"

"Last month when I read that Jericho thing. Abbie, I've got to run. By the time I do all my errands and get home, it'll be pitch dark."

"They're good for you, honey—if I couldn't look forward to a couple of hours a day with a good juicy romance, I'd have long since knocked off a whole boardful of directors, not to mention a certain administrator."

"Oh, goody. Then you'd have all the time in the world for reading romances, in between making license plates and busting rocks."

"I don't think they do that anymore," Abbie said, grinning as she ducked into her office to collect her coat and purse. "The trouble with you, Em, is that you give up too easily. So you were saddled with the girls and it broke up your engagement. Get out there and try again! Every woman worth her salt has a few broken romances behind her—it's part of the learning process."

As two sets of footsteps echoed hollowly along the empty corridor, Emily's eyes warmed in a tired smile. "I've already got an advanced degree, thanks. After Wendell, I fell for a man who decided to go back to his wife—and I didn't even know he had one—then there was Jonathan, my handsome weekend sailor. Actually, I was a part of a nervous breakdown he was having at the time, only I was too dumb to know it."

"So?"

"So I should throw my hat in the ring again and wait for another Prince Charming to pick it up?"

"You don't wait for him to pick it up, silly. If he looks good to you, you go put it in his hand. You might lose a few hats that way, but it beats the hell out of sitting home night after night grumbling about what other women are reading."

"Abbie, I honestly don't give a damn what you read—I think I'm just jealous. I've got two murder mysteries to review this weekend, and I *hate* murder mysteries! I always get a headache trying to remember all those tricky little clues, and I can never guess who dunit. I'd almost settle for another romance—at least whatever gets done, you know who did it."

"I wish you would—read one, that is. You know what they say about the physical benefits of owning a pet? Reading romances is even better—good for high blood pressure, ulcers, and whatever else ails you."

Holding the heavy front door open, Emily giggled. "I could never afford to read one now, not after this flap with B.J."

"Painted yourself into a corner, hmm? Believe me, it'd take more than all my four degrees put together to keep me from enjoying 'em."

"So that's it—I've only got two measly degrees. No wonder I don't appreciate good literature." Emily paused beside her car as the wind whipped her skirt against her slender legs. Her tan suit was ancient, but its pedigree was flawless.

"Did it ever occur to you, Em, that maybe you're in the wrong profession?"

"It's a little late to be discovering something like that, isn't it?" With a shrug and a smile, she slipped in under the wheel, hoping the loaner Bob had installed while he recharged her battery wouldn't let her down.

Abbie saw too much, she decided as the car started up obediently. Before she'd been jolted out of her half-formed plans for studying art in Rome, teaching had been pretty far down on her list of favorite occupations. But then she'd found herself with the girls to consider, and a teaching degree in English had seemed like a more realistic goal to shoot for. She'd never kidded herself about her moderate artistic talents.

The long drive home offered plenty of time to consider the question of her future. It was beginning to look as if one way or another, she might not have a job much longer. Given the opportunity, what would she like to do with the rest of her life?

A nebulous idea began to take shape in her mind. As long as she was fantasizing, she might as well admit that what she'd really like to do was to study. And not necessarily art. Now that she no longer had the heavy financial responsibility of the two girls, she'd give anything to be able to study all the fascinating subjects that had seemed too frivolous or impractical at the time. She'd almost forgotten what it was like to read a book for the pure pleasure of reading, and not because she had to write a review of it.

"And dammit, I'd like to put on my pajamas and eat chili and nachos from a paper plate in the living room while I watch the news, instead of forcing myself to go through the same old charade every night," she muttered belligerently as she turned into the leaf-covered driveway beside the cottage.

It was only generations of proud McClouds that

made her hold out so long. One of these days—on her fortieth birthday perhaps—she'd give in, she promised herself. Until then, she'd probably continue to maintain the standards that had been instilled in her from the cradle.

A shadow emerged from the porch, causing her heart to leap into her throat. "Emily, it's me—Bey. Sorry, I didn't mean to scare you."

"What are you *doing* here?" she demanded angrily, jamming the door key in the lock.

"I wanted to ask you something about a plant. I figure you know these woods better than anyone else."

"Are there any woods left?" she jeered. "My road's practically impassable, thanks to all those heavy vehicles you're using. By now you've probably bulldozed everything in sight."

She thrust open the door and began unbuttoning her coat, ignoring the way her heart was slamming against her ribs. At the continuing silence behind her, she snapped, "Well, what are you waiting for? Either come in or stay out, but please close the door."

He came in. Immediately the atmosphere was altered. The chilly room, with its scent of chrysanthemums and furniture polish, seemed to take on a new warmth that had nothing at all to do with temperature. The pungent scent of flowers was laced suddenly with an exotically masculine essence, and in spite of herself, Emily felt something inside her begin to thaw.

"Are you still camping out at the Landing?" she asked, her disgruntled tone in direct contrast to his cheerful response. She sounded like a shrew, and for the life of her, she couldn't seem to help it.

"Got there this morning. I couldn't wait any longer

to see how much house I had. The foundation's finished and they've started on the floor joists. By the end of next week I should have a floor and possibly even a wall or two. Now that the rock work's done, I've got two crews going." He made no effort to disguise his excitement, and Emily found the blend of tough competence and boyish eagerness utterly disarming.

Struggling to conceal her happiness at seeing him again, she lit the fire and then headed for the kitchen. Bey sauntered in after her, as friendly and relaxed as if their last meeting hadn't ended so ignominiously. She'd spend a week putting that miserable episode out of her mind.

"Would you like a cup of coffee?" Emily reached for the pot, not waiting for an answer. She needed one. In fact, she needed something stronger, but coffee would do for now.

They took it into the living room. Bey settled into the Morris chair as though by right. He was wearing jeans again, but this time they were black corduroy, soft and conforming. He wore a black wool pullover and the same boots he'd worn before—heavy, well-worn engineer's boots that made no pretense of being fashionable. He looked dark and dangerous, and every bit as attractive as she'd remembered, and Emily felt herself being drawn away from her safe shore and into deep, uncharted waters. "What was it you wanted to ask me?" she mumbled into her steaming cup.

"Did anyone ever live at Fletcher's Landing? I think there must have been a flower garden there at one time. I've got something blooming, and about the only flower I can identify is a rose—it's not a rose."

Between sips of coffee, Emily gave him a condensed version of the history of the place. "I haven't the slightest idea who lived there. By the time I was curious enough to ask, no one seemed to remember. At any rate, I don't think it was a McCloud, but I couldn't swear to it."

"And you've never seen the flowers?"

"Not from your description."

Carefully Bey placed his cup on a table. Rising, he took the poker and shook down the logs, releasing a shower of sparks. The resulting crackle sounded homey and pleasant to Emily's ears as she tucked her feet up beside her on the sofa.

"There's more than enough wood on there," she warned, remembering the last time. "That stack on the back porch is supposed to last until January."

"There's enough wood around here to last us both a lifetime. I'll have a fresh load stacked on your porch for you, all right?"

"I wasn't hinting, Bey. I just meant—"

"I know—I wasted three whole logs the other night. I'll replace 'em."

Impatiently she rattled her cup in her saucer. "I didn't *mean* that! Frankly, I'd much rather you left my share standing. A tree on the hoof is worth two in the fireplace."

"That's birds and bushes and hands."

Her lips twitched, but she managed to maintain a stern look. "Birds and bushes, too, please—especially those tall reeds with the silvery lavender tops."

"What about hands?"

"What about them?" Shifting her position so that

76

she could follow his movements, she made an effort to draw him out. "This corporation of yours, Bey—what does it do?"

He'd crossed the room to stand before the bookcase that took up almost an entire end of the room. The shelves were overflowing with books from her parents' library as well as the few she'd collected on her own. There was a tiny oil landscape on an easel, the only decent thing she'd ever done, between the encyclopedias and the history books.

Bey took it down, studied it silently for several moments, and then carefully replaced it. Ignoring her question, he continued to examine the shelves. Emily continued to examine him, her eyes traveling slowly over the back of his well-shaped head and the wide black-clad shoulders. She could see the hollow of his spine and the indentation of his waist just above where his jeans were belted low on his narrow hips. He'd moved as silently as a cat burglar in those heavy boots, but somehow, despite her earlier fears, she knew she could trust him. There was a disarming directness about him, a steadiness of eye that was reassuring. Whatever else he was, Bey Jones was no threat to her possessions.

As to her peace of mind, that was another matter. If he were a book, she decided with instinctive certainty, she'd be compelled to read him; the cover was so irresistibly intriguing.

He turned before she could disguise her interest, and for a long moment their eyes clung. If she were an imaginative sort, she might have read all sorts of things in the quick darkening of those amber-and-emerald eyes.

He leaned against the bookcase, crossing his arms over his chest. "These books don't fit you, Emily. Too dry."

"I happen to be a dry sort of person."

"Like hell you are." His skeptical tone served to sharpen the awareness between them until she was all but trembling. "Suppressed, maybe . . . inhibited, probably . . . but dry? Never."

She felt as if she'd downed a glass of champagne too quickly. "Interesting conclusion, Bey," she observed coolly, "but you're wrong on all three counts."

"Shall I prove which one of us is wrong?"

She did her best to sound uninterested. "Don't bother. The opinion of strangers has never concerned me overmuch. If you want to believe I'm . . . all those things you said, then be my guest."

With a swift shift of direction that left her slightly off balance, he asked, "What do you like to read?"

"Lately I haven't had much time to read anything— at least not for pleasure."

She followed his movements as he prowled about the room. He had an efficient way of walking that used a minimum of effort. She watched him scan the shelves once more. His eyes lingered for a moment on the painting, and then he crossed to stand before her, feet apart, lean torso settling into a deceptively relaxed stance.

Her gaze focused on the hands that were resting on his hips. Against the darkness of his clothing, the crisp golden hair on their backs seemed incandescent. Those hard, muscular forearms might well belong to a fighter, but his square, well-kept hands seemed more suited to . . .

An unaccountable warmth crept up her body, and she moved restlessly, dismissing the irrelevant thought. He'd carefully avoided her direct question about who he was and what he did, she noticed. The more she saw of the man, the more of an enigma he became.

He stood before her, casually blocking any attempt at escape she might have made. The slow smile that spread across his craggy face had the effect of cutting through every protective layer she possessed, and she found herself totally defenseless.

"I thought we might have lunch tomorrow," he said, his resonant voice registering on the very marrow of her bones. "I owe you. Would twelve, twelve-thirty suit you?"

Emily broke away from the magnetism of his gaze. Huskily she said, "You don't have to—"

"Of course, if you've got other plans . . ."

"Well, if you're sure—"

"Fine. Pick you up about twelve-fifteen." He reached out and cupped her cheek with the hard palm of his hand, and Emily waited breathlessly for it to burst into flames. The hand dropped, and helplessly she watched him move toward the door. "I'd better go get a fire built if I want to eat tonight. See you tomorrow."

Long after he'd let himself out, she sat staring at the door, feeling as if she'd been buffeted by a small tornado. What on earth was she doing accepting a lunch date with someone like Bey Jones? What would they talk about? How would they get to town—on the back of his motorcycle? She'd never been on one of those things in her life, and she had decidedly mixed feelings about roaring through the countryside with nothing to hang on to but the driver.

By the time she heard the rap on her front door, she'd changed clothes three times, settling finally on navy wool slacks and a green turtleneck sweater. That would do for lunch in any restaurant in any of the nearby towns, as well as for her first ride on a motorcycle. For added confidence, she wore her high-heeled navy suede boots. No man liked to be seen with a woman who was taller than he was, and she needed all the help she could get.

It wasn't enough. Bey greeted her with that incongruously guileless smile of his, and she felt herself sinking once again under his potent spell.

"You're beautiful in green. Brings out the color in your face," he told her, opening her closet as if he had every right and extracting the suede jacket.

The color in her face had nothing at all to do with her green sweater. Emily allowed herself to be helped on with the coat, wondering why she'd ever thought she could intimidate him with a few additional inches. Bey was probably no more than five-feet-ten, but he radiated more confidence and more power than any basketball star she'd ever seen. He was in complete control of himself, and as a result, Emily felt her own confidence begin to ebb before they'd even left the house.

"Where's the motorcycle?" she asked, glancing around for the black-and-white machine.

Bey took her arm and angled through the yard toward the woods. "Left it home. Maybe I'll build a garage for it one of these days. Could double as a doghouse if I decide to get a dog, speaking of which, I hope you like hotdogs. I considered grilling a couple of steaks, but I've only got one steak knife—the one I use to measure coffee."

"We're picnicking?" Despite her slightly longer legs, their strides matched perfectly. Bey held aside a small branch until she'd passed.

"You don't want to? We could run into town if you'd rather, but I'll have to douse the fire first." The hint of disappointment in his voice struck a nerve she didn't even know she possessed, and she hurriedly assured him that there was nothing she'd rather have than a campfire meal.

They walked silently, their feet scuffling a path through the carpet of red and golden leaves. A jay announced their coming, his raucous voice echoing in the silence.

"I envy you," Emily said wistfully.

"All this?" He gestured around him, and she nodded. His hand moved to hers as they came to the half-rotted trunk of a pine that had died of old age. They stepped over, and he continued to hold her hand. "It'll always be yours, Emily. A little thing like a deed can't change that."

The glowing ambience of the deep woods and the warmth of his touch combined to bring an unexpected ache deep inside her. She pulled her hand away and increased her pace. "I'm hungry," she announced brightly. "Starved, in fact."

"Great. You're my first houseguest, and I'm going to treat you right. There's a wheelbarrow around here somewhere—the rock masons used it—so feel free to pig out: if you overdo it, I can still get you home."

They were nearing the place where she'd discovered him that first day, and she began to see signs of construction. Critically she glanced around. "I don't see any sign of a road. How have the trucks been getting in and out?"

"The long way. I didn't want to tear up the area between your place and mine, so I routed them around near the water. Come on, we're almost there. I spent the morning cleaning up for you, but I'm afraid it's still a little messy."

They came to the clearing a few moments later, and Emily uttered a soft cry of dismay. Smoke from the campfire drifted lazily upward, but no amount of smoke could disguise the raw wounds in what had once been untouched forest. There were mounds of bare earth and splotches of rough, hardened concrete. There was a small mountain of gravel, a scattering of rock, and stacks of assorted building materials underneath the gaping hole in the canopy of trees overhead. Deep, muddy tire tracks were everywhere, and centering the small clearing was the foundation of a house not much larger than her own.

"I'm sorry," Bey said quietly. He was standing beside her, his arms hanging limply at his side. Distress was plain in his eyes, and Emily shook her head.

"No—I'm the one who's sorry. Bey, it's your land. I can't expect you to turn it into a wildlife sanctuary."

"There's a lot of land here, Emily. The wounds will heal over, and the house will blend in. God knows the last thing I want is to stick out like a sore thumb. One of the reasons I wanted this place was for the privacy it offered."

The initial shock was wearing off, and Emily picked her way through the sticky mud and approached the rock foundation. "How about a guided tour?"

Bey leapt up to and turned to give her a hand. "It'll

be easier to visualize after the floor's done. Watch your step in those heels."

Holding on to her hand, he pointed out various undefined areas as kitchen, bedroom, study and bath. "The chimney's this big slab here—fireplaces in every room but the bath. I couldn't figure out a way to get a fireplace in there."

"Cozy," she murmured, distracted by the feel of the hard hand enclosing her own. She'd never dreamed that the feel of flesh against flesh could be so catalytic. "What about a living room?" she asked shakenly.

"Oh, well—I thought this area over here could serve as den, study, library, living room, office—you name it. No point in spreading out over half an acre."

They discussed the house plans, arguing amicably for several minutes, and then Bey leapt down and lifted his arms. "You said you were starved. For the time being, my dining room's that small clearing over there."

She was no more than three feet off the ground, but the invitation was irresistible. Leaning forward, she placed her hands on his shoulders and jumped. The ground was uneven. Her heels sank into the soft earth, and she stumbled, laughing breathlessly. When his arms closed around her, she had time to give only a small whimper of protest.

5

Bey turned, still holding her in his arms, and seated them on a sheet of plywood that covered a section of floor joists. Using his strength with incredible finesse, he eased her down onto the fragrant raw wood, and then leaned over her, bracing himself with one arm to gaze down at her face. Her hair flowed around her like dark threads of gold-shot silk, and those cheekbones, those eyes—ah, she was so beautiful, so distant and yet so familiar, like some half-remembered dream from another life.

Disarming her first with a kindling smile, he began gently grazing the corners of her mouth with small kisses, straying now and then to brush the tip of her nose with his lips. Emily held her breath. A cool wine-colored leaf drifted down onto her forehead, and still smiling, Bey pressed his lips against it, holding it to her heated skin for a moment.

"There, now you're wearing my brand," he murmured deeply.

"Bey . . ." A little frantically she searched for a handhold on reality, but reason had deserted her, her wits scattering out of reach like the flurries of wind-blown leaves. Before she could help herself, she was entangled again in the splendor of his eyes, lost in a thicket of russet lashes that reflected in his irises like brambles in a hidden woodland pool.

Intellectually she would never on this earth have put herself willingly into the hands of a man like Bey. It was an admission of vulnerability, and vulnerability led to disillusionment and pain. After the example set for her by her parents, after the fiasco of her own engagement, she'd taken care to build up an impervious defense against the sort of power an attractive man could wield over a lonely woman. And now, at the first test . . .

Intellectually she was immune, but emotionally she was as defenseless as ever.

Emily surrendered herself to the spell of Bey's hungry lips. He was kissing her with a barely controlled fierceness that should have been frightening, but somehow wasn't. In danger of being torn apart by the conflicting demands of mind and body, she simply ceased thinking. It was treacherously easy just to give herself up to the depradations of that sweet, firm mouth, the comfort of those hard, sheltering arms.

She trembled under the slow, gentle movement of his hand as it smoothed its way inside her jacket, under her sweater, to stroke the soft skin just above her waist. The heat of their combined bodies released the intoxicating scent of leather, of warm flesh, of her cologne, and something that was richly masculine.

Breathing deeply, she drew it into her consciousness to weave it into the shimmering tapestry of this moment out of time.

And it was only a moment, she reminded herself distractedly. It could sparkle and beguile, but then it would end, and once more she'd be . . . Emily. Lonely, unsparkling, unbeguiling Emily.

Bey's mouth fitted itself to hers, and his tongue began probing the curved line between her lips, as if searching out weaknesses. One hand wandered up over her shoulder, tantalizing the side of her breast in passing, and the warning disintegrated like fog under sunlight. His fingers curled into the neckline of her sweater, seeking the perfumed warmth of her throat. They strayed up to the satin skin of her chin, sensitively delineating the delicate bones of her jaw, the defenseless softness beneath. With thumb and forefinger he pried her jaws apart, quickly moving to consolidate his gain by deepening the kiss before she could protest.

As if she had the strength of will to protest something she'd craved without even realizing it. Emily prided herself that self-delusion was not among her failings.

His tongue explored the smooth edges of her teeth, the inside of her lips. It engaged its counterpart in a slow, erotic dance that had her fingers clutching mindlessly at the taut muscles of his back. She could feel his body growing hard and tense over hers, and the knowledge of his arousal was electrifying. His breath grew increasingly ragged as her fevered response had her twisting and arching beneath him. And then, when every nerve in her body was screaming for release, he drew back, disengaging her clutching hands, her reaching arms.

Cool air rushed between them, and she stared up at him, bewildered. With an unsteady hand Bey raked back his thick sun-streaked hair. His next words struck her with an almost ludicrous sense of incongruity. "I expect that fire's burned down enough by now," he said huskily. "Shall we go see about some food?"

Emily plummeted to earth and landed without actually breaking anything. Sitting up, she brushed a wood shaving from her sweater and, forcing a commendable degree of composure into her voice, said, "Oh, yes—please. I'm starving."

The look he shot her spoke volumes, and she felt the heat rush up to redden her translucent complexion. Abruptly turning away, she slipped off her jacket and draped it over a stack of two-by-fours. *It was a kiss, you silly fool—a casual kiss, that's all! People do it all the time.*

But there'd been nothing faintly casual about it. How far it would have gone, she'd never know, but she certainly hadn't been putting up much of a fight. The thought was acutely embarrassing. Arranging her hair into some semblance of order, she glanced across to where Bey was bending over the fire. Was he paler than usual, or was she imagining things?

The hotdogs were superb, burned to a crisp on the outside, succulent and bursting with flavor on the inside. Bey loaded her bun with slaw and chili from plastic containers. He sliced a red onion and layered it generously and then splashed on a mustard that was all but combustible.

By the time he served the first round, Emily had

regained her perspective. So she was out of practice; that was no reason to get carried away by a simple kiss.

"I planned on three apiece," Bey informed her. "Then we'll see about dessert."

Sending him a skeptical look, she opened wide and bit off a chunk, closing her eyes in appreciation. Moments later, she was blinking away tears. "Is there a fire extinguisher handy? Bey, if I manage even one of these monsters my insurance rates will double."

"Fire or medical?" He sat cross-legged on a slab of wood, having given Emily the seat of honor, a rough carpenter's stool.

"Both, but it'll be worth it. They're scrumptious."

They continued to eat in silence, and Emily gazed around at the tall hardwoods. The leaves were going fast now; a few more weeks and they'd be gone. Her eyes strayed to the yellow one-man tent pitched some hundred feet away. Surely he wouldn't camp out here in the dead of winter? Trees or not, the wind that whipped in off the bay could be ferocious.

The question died on her lips as she turned and caught the unguarded expression on his face. He was staring at the rock foundation with a look of raw longing mixed with disbelief, and once again Emily was shaken by the complexity of Bey Jones.

"Bey, who are you, anyway?" she asked softly, feeling oddly like an intruder as her words broke through his preoccupation.

"What do you mean, who am I?" There was an unexpected edge to his voice.

"I only meant—what do you do? Where do you come from?"

"I told you about Bon-Bey. As to where I come from—"

"No, you didn't. Do you realize that I know more about the UPS delivery man than I do about you? *What* and *where* is Bon-Bey?" She waited impatiently as he loaded another bun and held it out to her. The man was a master of evasion. Maybe he was an escaped convict. Maybe he was an illegal alien, or a spy. What better place to hide out?

She wrenched her mind back from its fanciful suppositions and reached for the wiener. "You'd better have that wheelbarrow handy," she taunted.

"I can always throw you over my saddle and carry you home that way. Or you could stay and be my first—"

"Houseguest? Thanks, but I'll manage to waddle home somehow. You were saying?"

"Yeah. Well, I guess you'd say Bon-Bey is concerned primarily with publishing. And as for where I come from, Baltimore's as good an answer as any. I've bedded down in a lot of places in my thirty-two years, but I always seem to find my way back there.

"You're only thirty-two?" Somehow he'd seemed much older. And yet, in spite of the occasional flashes of boyishness, Bey possessed a sort of tough maturity she'd seen in few other men. Disconcerted, she lifted her eyes to find him studying her with a maddening smile.

"Any objections?" He lifted one russet brow, and she tore her eyes away and poked at an escaping onion with a mustardy finger.

"Of course not. Your age is nothing to do with me."

"How old are you?" He reached for the carton and

divided what was left of the milk into the two enameled mugs.

"If you go around asking questions like that, I'm surprised you've survived this long." She grinned, took a large bite, and then fanned her face. By the time she could swallow, tears were streaming down her cheeks. "It's good, though," she assured him, gratefully accepting his milk after she'd downed her own. "I'm thirty-seven," she admitted candidly.

Nodding thoughtfully, Bey wolfed down the last of his second hotdog and began spreading another bun with condiments. "Sounds about right to me," he murmured, cutting into a fresh onion with his sheath knife. It occurred to Emily that it was probably the one he used to measure coffee.

"About right for what?"

"Us. That's a mean difference of two and a half years. Physiologically speaking, it would be better if I were a few years younger or you were maybe forty, but I don't anticipate any trouble."

Bemused, Emily laid down her unfinished hotdog and stood up. Forcing a note of exasperation to cover the rush that had come over her at his calm declaration, she said, "I don't anticipate any trouble either, as a matter of fact, not that our respective ages have any significance. Even when I lived in town, I was never particularly neighborly, so chances are we won't be seeing all that much of each other."

After carefully balancing a long strip of kosher dill pickle on top of his bulging bun, Bey turned his attention to the part of her that was nearest—her boots. His gaze rambled thoughtfully up the length of her legs, encased in navy wool flannel that was now slightly less than pristine. As she'd dispensed with her jacket earlier, there was nothing at all to protect her from the thorough survey as his eyes lingered on the swell of her breasts before finally moving on to her increasingly angry face.

"You were saying . . . ?" He took a large bite of his third hotdog and chewed thoughtfully as he awaited her answer.

"Dammit, Bey, don't play cat and mouse with me!"

His eyes widened ingenuously. "Is that what you think I'm doing?"

"I don't play games," she said adamantly. "Look, I think we'd better level with each other. This has been lovely, but we're even now. I gave you dinner; you gave me lunch. We've traded courtesies, so let's quit while we're ahead. Quite frankly, I don't think we have anything at all in common except for the fact that we're neighbors."

"I must say, I like your idea of courtesy. I'll trade with you any day."

By the time she could come up with an annihilating retort, he seemed to have forgotten her presence. There was an odd expression in his eyes, one that might even have been called dreamy if it weren't for the twice-broken nose, the pugnacious chin, the formidable jawline and that "damn-your-hide" arrogance he wore so carelessly.

"That's *it!*" he murmured under his breath. Rolling to his feet with a swift agility that took her by surprise, he stuck out his hand. "Sure you won't stay for dessert?"

Not even to herself could Emily admit her dismay at what amounted to a brush-off. "No thanks," she said coolly, ignoring the extended hand. "It's been delightful—thank you for inviting me . . . but I'd better be getting home—a million and one things to do, you know." If her small laugh sounded more brittle than carefree, it was the best she could manage at the moment.

"Yeah, well . . . thanks for coming, Emily. I'll see you. *Soon.*"

Don't count on it, Emily thought strickenly as she hurried away from the campsite. Blind, for once, to the beauty of the woods she'd loved all her life, she couldn't wait to escape them, to shut herself up in her bedroom and cry herself sick.

Which was precisely what she did, for no good reason other than that she couldn't help herself. Every woman, she thought brokenly, deserves a good cry once in a blue moon. Even the non-criers. She was a non-crier herself—had been, that is, until she'd run headlong into a young barbarian who'd made confetti of her defenses without even trying.

Some half-hour later she stood before the bookshelf and tried to see it through the eyes of a stranger. She lifted the small landscape from its easel and studied it, wondering if Bey had noticed the tiny "E. McC." in the lower-left corner. It was a study she'd done years ago of the ruined wharf at the Landing. There was hardly anything left of the ancient pilings and rotted timbers by now.

Dry? Her eyes scanned the shelves, wondering how they reflected on the owner. There was a preponderance of reference books. Ansie had given away most of the modern fiction when they'd moved from the house to the much smaller apartment in Easton. Emily had relied on the public library until she'd grown too busy to read for pleasure.

He'd called her inhibited and suppressed, as if he were an expert on women. The egotism of some men was astounding.

Aimlessly she opened the enormous dictionary. Her gaze fell to the middle of the randomly chosen page. *Barbarian; foreign, primitive, savage.* He was definitely foreign to her limited experience, as different from Wendell and the other men she'd known as a kitten was from a cougar. Primitive? In a sense. There was a basic earthiness about the man that was both appealing and frightening. Savage? Probably—given reason.

Sighing, she closed the dictionary. Whatever he was—*whoever* he was—there was no room in her orderly existence for a man like Bey Jones. He was too young, for one thing. Or she was too old. And anyway, they had absolutely nothing in common.

Emily spent the rest of the afternoon struggling through the first of the two murder mysteries she was expected to review. Clue after clue slipped through her fingers as her attention strayed back to the woods, to the building site. He might be gone by now for all she knew. Or maybe he had someone else there with him. He'd certainly tired of her own company quickly enough—couldn't wait to get rid of her. But then, the young had such a short attention span, she rationalized desperately.

She slammed the book shut and stood up. Dammit, it wasn't fair for him to barge into her life and disrupt everything just because he wanted to show off his new house! She had better things to do with her time.

Reaching for the phone, she dialed Abbie Linga's number. After the tenth ring, she hung up. She needed to get out. A movie would be just the thing to get her out of this maudlin mood, but she didn't relish going by herself. That was the trouble with living alone; all your friends were married and had families, or had moved away. When you suddenly had a craving to go to a movie, there was no one around.

Not allowing herself time to think, she dialed Wendell's home number. Nancy Roscoe answered.

"Oh, hi, Nancy. How was Italy?"

"It was Greece, and I adored it. Em? Thought I recognized your voice. If you wanted to speak to Wendell, he's in the shower. Can I take a message?"

Emily held the phone away from her ear and grimaced. Now, why would he be taking a shower at five-thirty in the afternoon? "Oh, it was nothing—just something about the book reviews. It can wait."

She hung up the phone and stood there wrapping her arms about herself and staring down at a torn and muddy leaf she'd tracked in. The scent of dead ashes filled the room as a gust of wind stirred the hearth. Suddenly she felt utterly alone in the world, and it was frightening. Alone was such a desolate place to be.

"Dammit, I refuse to be depressed over a silly, meaningless incident!" she muttered ferociously. Stalking into her bedroom, she changed into her oldest clothes. It would be dark before she could do much more than drag the ladder out and put it into place, but there were shutters to be painted, storm windows to be put up, and all the gutters were overflowing with leaves. And for once she was positively brimming with energy. She *had* to do something physical, or she'd never manage to sleep tonight, and besides, she could use a feeling of accomplishment about now.

Squatting on the cold ground, Bey scribbled furiously for three-quarters of an hour, his scowl gradually giving way to a grin of satisfaction. It had been there all along, buried under the superficial layers of his mind, but he'd been blind to it. He'd been struggling for two weeks with his damned Belinda and she'd persistently refused to behave.

And no damned wonder. He'd been trying to force her into a form that was all wrong. The petite green-eyed blonde with the sultry voice and a knowing way with men had been patterned on a woman he'd been briefly involved with. Della was a feature writer for a Baltimore paper, and Bey had severed the relationship when she'd started asking too many questions about how he made his money and what he did with his time when they weren't together. It had occurred to him later that she probably thought he was a dealer in something highly illicit.

Della had been a likely enough candidate for heroinehood. Volatile, intelligent, attractive, she'd have made a good one, only somehow, in the process of getting her down on paper, she'd undergone a slow metamorphosis. He'd fought it because he hadn't understood what was happening, but now that his Belinda had finally evolved into a tall, gray-eyed, brown-haired woman with breeding and integrity in every bone of her body, he felt an enormous sense of relief. The plot all fell into place now that his heroine had come to life.

Something else was beginning to emerge in his consciousness as well, and he made a deliberate effort to put a lid on it. He'd almost gotten in over his head today, and he couldn't afford the luxury. Not yet. With a woman like Emily, it paid to take it slow and easy—if one took it at all.

Forcing his attention back to the written word, Bey nodded thoughtfully. "Skim off the dross and we get down to the gold. Play the gold against the steel and we've got the story." With a crooked grin of triumph, he capped the pen and rammed it into his shirt pocket and then riffled through the pages of his small notebook. A frown quickly replaced the look of satisfaction. Three pages left. Three small pages!

Softly and with deadly efficiency he swore. He'd sooner have been caught out here in the dead of winter in nothing but his skivvies than without enough writing materials. Ideas popped into his head at the damnedest times, and he went crazy if he couldn't get them down.

It meant another trip into town. It was practically dark, and he had a hell of a lot of thinking to do. He'd planned to crawl into his mummy bag and mull over a few things during that creative period between the time when his mind went into overdrive and the time he fell asleep.

Leaning over, he grabbed the bucket of water he always kept handy and emptied it onto the ashes of his fire. And then, for the first time since Emily had left him, he stood up.

Damn—he was stiff as a board! Thirty-two might sound young to some people, but he'd got a hell of a lot of mileage out of every one of those years.

He headed for the tent, where he'd left his keys, and it was then that he saw Emily's brown suede jacket. Veering toward the lumber pile, he hooked it with one hand and brought it up to his face. As he inhaled her fragrance, a slow smile gentled his rugged features. God, what a woman. Talk about your dross and your gold . . . !

Whistling loudly in an effort that was more bravado than bravura, Emily hung on to the broom handle with one hand and the gutter with the other as she balanced on next to the top rung. She could hardly see as far as the corner of the roof, but she was determined to finish what she'd started. She needed the satisfaction of finishing at least one thing today. The reports could wait another week; the school might fold before anyone got around to reading them anyway. But at least her gutters would be clean. She'd learned a long time ago to take pleasure in small triumphs when the larger ones eluded her.

She didn't see him round the corner just as the last streak of pale pink light faded from the western sky. The first she knew that she wasn't alone was the rasping oath that assaulted her ears.

"Judas priest, woman, would you tell me just what the hell you think you're doing up there?"

Startled, she twisted around. The rusty metal gutter protested noisily as it sagged under her gripping fingers. "Bey?" she squeaked.

"Are you crazy? Wait—don't move!"

It was too late. She felt the ladder begin to lean, and she clutched at the roof, only there was nothing to hold on to. "Get away, get away," she screamed, as the world lurched past her. In the split second before she landed, she made an effort to relax, recalling fragments of something she'd read about the proper way to fall.

The falling was fine; there was nothing at all proper about the landing, however. She felt herself literally plucked out of the air by two incredibly strong arms, and then she was sprawling all over a mass of warm granite.

It was several long moments before she could think, much less move. By the time she came to her senses, she was horribly aware of the still form beneath her. "Bey? Oh, God, Bey, I've broken you," she wailed, easing herself to her knees.

She placed a hand on his chest. It was too dark to see clearly, but it was definitely a chest under her palm. And it was definitely not working properly. Broken phrases of concern were interspersed with unconvincing ones of reassurance as she placed her ear just over his mouth.

He wasn't breathing.

"Oh, my God . . ." Heartbeat—clear the air passages—expand the lungs. Fragments of the CPR routine filtered into her shocked mind as she maneuvered herself into position and cupped his chin with one hand. Her mouth covered his slack lips, and then she remembered to shut off the nasal air passage. Lifting her head slightly, she was struggling to support his neck and pinch his nose when he began to stir.

A reedy gasp struck her ear and he muttered, "Forget the nose, love—it's the mouth that's important."

"Bey! Oh, Bey, you're alive!" Crumpling, she rested her forehead on his chest as her knees dug deeper into the frost-softened earth. She was dimly aware of the dampness permeating her jeans, and acutely aware of the rock-hardness of the chest under her face. She felt a hand come up to stroke the back of her hair, and Bey's voice, for once distinctly lacking in strength, murmured, "You okay, Emily? Nothing broken, I hope."

Lifting her head, she laughed shakily. "I thought you were. Didn't you hear my warning?"

Still holding her face against his chest, Bey sat up. The positions were awkward, but neither of them seemed to notice. "Didn't you hear mine?" he shot back weakly.

"By then it was too late. Next time I'll yell 'Timber.'" Her hands moved restlessly over his shoulders and arms for reassurance. "That darned ladder— I knew the ground was too soft on this side of the house. I finished all the others, though, and I only wanted to . . . Bey, what are you doing here?" She was still on her knees, off balance as his arms held her tightly to him. In no condition to fight gravity, she lowered her hips to the ground, her legs trailing across his thighs.

"Came to return your jacket," he murmured warmly into her hair. "I think I threw it over by that green thing with the red berries."

"Yew," she whispered, fitting herself more closely to the hollow of his shoulder.

"Yes?" His voice was a resonance that vibrated all the way to the base of her spine.

"What?"

"What were you going to say?"

"When?"

"You said *you*," he reminded her, examining her vertebrae with gentle expertise.

"That's what it is—my jacket. The bush."

"Did you land on your head?" His lips brushed over

her cheek and burned against the side of her cold nose. Helplessly she raised her head, and with a soft groan he took her mouth.

Her lips parted at the first touch of his thrusting tongue, and he lowered his back to the ground, bringing her down on top of him. One of her hands pressed into the soft, cold ground for balance; the other found its way under his black sweater. His flesh was warm and resilient, and she kneaded it feverishly as his hungry mouth unleashed a wild response deep inside her.

She had on too many clothes. Her breasts craved the touch of his hands, of his bare flesh, but they were separated by too many layers of wool and cotton and nylon. His hand moved to her hips, cupping and stroking before shifting her so that she was lying full length on top of him.

A soft startled groan emerged from the depths of her throat. Oh, God, it was starting all over again. *This was insane.* She hardly even knew him—he was years younger than she was, and she was on fire for him.

Bey's hand moved under her sweater, under the flannel shirt she wore beneath it, and slipped between the hardness of his own chest and the softness of her throbbing breast. There had to be a better way—

He rolled over, still holding her tightly against him. His mouth trailed hot, moist kisses from her lips to the hollow under her cheekbone, to her temple. "I want you so much I'm half-crazy, Emily." The slow, agonized emphasis on each word raked trails of liquid fire through her body. "I didn't mean this to happen so soon, darling, but I . . . It's too late now."

The hot rush of his breath against her ear, the intoxicating taste of him, the feel of his powerfully aroused body against hers—these sensations unwillingly gave way to other, less pleasant ones. Emily's clothing had twisted under her, and a stretch of bare skin was slowly freezing in the night air. Cold dampness was seeping through the thin layer of her jeans, and assorted aches and stiffnesses were beginning to clamor for attention.

Under the circumstances, it was relatively easy for her to back away from the volatile situation. She was just lucky it hadn't happened on a warm summer night when she was wearing next to nothing. She began to disengage herself, slightly chagrined when he let her go without an argument.

"Bey, I don't know about you, but I'm freezing to death—and I think I might have sprained my foot. Is that possible? A foot?"

He sat up again, expelling his breath in a deep, shuddering sigh. "Yeah, I guess it's possible to sprain almost anything."

She got to her feet, gingerly testing the left one before applying any weight on it. Quickly shifting to her right one, she began flexing her arms and fingers. "What about you? Any injuries? Good Lord, I landed on top of you, and I'm no butterfly."

"I must have sprained my judgement," he said wryly. "Believe it or not, I don't normally pounce on women the minute the sun goes down."

Laughing breathlessly, Emily touched her throat. "At least there are no puncture wounds." Turning toward the back door, she added, "And in this particular instance, I did the pouncing. Come on inside where it's warm, Bey."

"Yeah, well . . . just long enough to be sure you're okay, then I'll be on my way." He followed her around the corner of the house, and in the darkness she couldn't tell if he was limping or not. She was. She'd whacked her foot good, and sneakers weren't much protection.

"I could do with a cup of coffee," she chattered through clenched teeth. It was something other than the falling temperature that had locked her muscles into painful rigidity.

Snapping on the overhead light, she turned away, struggling for composure. She heard the scrape of a chair, and a sound that was half-sigh, half-groan. Averting her eyes, she busied herself with filling the coffee maker with water and then paused, gripping the edge of the counter.

Lord, how could she ever face him after wallowing around on the ground that way? As if she hadn't made a fool of herself once today, already. His hands had roamed all over her, and both times she'd permitted it. Permitted it—she'd *loved* it! Even after that peremptory brush-off he'd handed her today.

Dumping coffee recklessly into the filter, she wondered how she'd managed to delude herself all these years as to her own sensual nature. With Wendell she'd rationalized her disappointment as inexperience. With Bo, it had been a certain lack of openness that had prevented her from drifting into a physical relationship. Later, of course, she'd been glad it had never progressed that far.

And Jonathan—handsome, charming, romantic Jonathan. He'd been every woman's ideal lover, up to a point. And then at that point he'd been a failure, and he'd blamed his failure on her. And by the time she'd come to realize that his problems were deep-seated and of long standing, she'd felt so sorry for him that she'd accepted the blame. The day he'd sailed out of her life on his sleek forty-five-foot yawl had been the day she'd put all nonsense about men and romance out of her life.

"You're limping," Bey accused, breaking into her thoughts.

The coffee gurgled peacefully, and Emily took down two delicate cups, wishing for once she had a pair of heavy utilitarian mugs to wrap her cold hands around.

Adjusting a determined smile on her face, she turned to deny the charge. "No I'm not. I'm fine, just fine. I think maybe my foot was just frozen."

"Take off your shoe and let me see."

"Look, Bey, if you want coffee, just sit quietly until it's finished making, drink it and then go," she said evenly. "I'm not hurt, and I'm not taking off anything."

He settled back into the chair, his arms spreading along the armrests and his legs stretching out across her polished pine floor. The crooked grin that creased his cheeks and sparkled in his eyes did nothing at all to reassure her.

"Sooner or later, you will, you know. But I can wait. I want it to be the proper time and place."

6

Wearily raking a hand through his unruly hair, Bey shoved his chair away from the desk. Pulling out of his story after a long work session was like coming out of an afternoon movie; one was always surprised to discover that the rest of the world was still out there.

For four eighteen-hour days, he'd been subsisting on his usual fare of black coffee, beer and Vienna sausages. His jeans hung on his bones like the hide on a starving hound, but he'd written three chapters, rough-editing with pencil at the end of each session. At this rate he'd be ready to negotiate by the middle of November.

He could use the advance; buying the property had knocked the starch out of his bank account, and the house was eating into his funds faster than he'd expected. He had a few good investments that paid monthly dividends, but otherwise, it was feast or famine. Royalty checks twice a year, and an advance when he mailed in a book.

It was a hell of a way to make a living, but he was hooked—he'd wanted to be a writer ever since he'd read his first western. Of course, if he'd stuck to westerns, he wouldn't be where he was today. On the other hand, he wouldn't have to be so damned secretive about what he did for a living.

He glanced around him, wondering if he had anything in the house to eat. God, what a cheerless room. He'd deliberately downplayed any sign of affluence, not wanting to arouse the hunting instincts of some of his more unsavory aquaintances, but maybe he'd overdone it.

If word got out that he could have bought the whole damned building as a tax write-off, he'd have been ripe for plucking by every small-time hood in the neighborhood. And if he got ripped off and registered a complaint about it, he'd have to answer a few questions. He didn't care to have to explain the source of his income to some hard-nosed cop.

He stood up and stretched, flexing the muscles of his back and shoulders. He could do with some fresh air and a bowl of chili, maybe some doughnuts or a few of the Kahlua brownies he'd developed a taste for. He'd been cooped up for four days, and the first day hadn't been all that productive. He'd had a hell of a time focusing his mind on his work.

Emily McCloud. It was the right name for her, he mused. Bey had an instinct for names. Sometimes it took him more time to find the right name for his heroine than it did to decide on her career. Emily was . . . Emily. And unfortunately, he was more inter-ested in furthering the relationship between Emily and Bey than he was the one between Belinda and Cain.

He was almost out the door when the phone rang. For two bits he'd have ignored it. Chances were pretty good, though, that it was either his agent or his editor. Not many people knew his number, and he wasn't in the book.

He growled into the instrument.

"Hello, love, want to take me to a party?" a familiar voice crooned.

Bey's lips tightened. He'd all but told the woman to get lost six months ago. What did it take to make it stick? "Am I the best you could do, Della?"

"You're the best any woman could do, darling . . . only I haven't done you lately."

"Crudeness doesn't become a woman, Della. What did you want?"

A musical laugh shimmered against his ear. "That's what I adore about you, Beyard, you're such a lovely bundle of contradictions—that old-fashioned chauvin-ism that pops up when I least expect it. I wonder what that macho facade of yours is *really* covering up?"

"At the moment it's covering up an empty belly. I was on my way out the door to get a bowl of chili, so why don't we cut this little visit short, huh?"

"Oh, goody! Our old place? I'll meet you there. I've got some interesting gossip to—"

"Della, gossip gives me indigestion."

"I haven't seen you since I covered this convention in D.C. a few months back—romance writers. Hun-dreds of 'em, and agents and editors swarming all over the place. I'm beginning to think I'm in the wrong end of the writing business. And, Bey—some of the rumors I heard will amuse you."

"I seriously doubt it," Bey said dryly. His eyes narrowed and the planes of his face flattened imperceptibly as he waited for her to get to the point. Della never wasted time on idle gossip unless she was ferreting.

"Are you still there? Darling, it was fascinating. The women who write these things—would you believe that some of them are lawyers, librarians, pilots—even journalists? I met an English prof from some university or other who writes one a year—the torrid kind."

"Is that it? Della, I hate to cut you off, but—"

As though he hadn't interrupted her, the lilting voice went on to say, "But you know what I found the most fascinating, darling? Some of the writers—not many, but a few—are men using women's names. I actually met two of them, and they're . . . mmmmm, well let's just say I'd *adore* helping them with their research."

"Good luck," Bey replied calmly.

"But about this party, Bey, it's—"

"Della, look, I've got to run. I'm leaving town this afternoon, and I don't know exactly when I'll be back. Thanks for the invitation, but you know how I feel about parties."

"I haven't forgotten, my charming misfit. You hate people, you despise socializing, and you can't stand frivolity—except when it comes to women's lingerie." She ignored his snort of disgust to continue breezily, "Well, darling, if you'd rather have a private party, you know where I live."

"Della, I just told you I was on my way out of town."

"More government business?" she purred. He'd mentioned once, when her inquisitive mind had backed him into a corner, that he'd done some work for the government a few years back and that he still had to be ready to leave town at a moment's notice.

Which was literally the truth. Four years in the army qualified as government work by anyone's standards. And when a beautiful green-eyed blonde started digging into matters that didn't concern her, he'd found it expedient to get out of town. One of the reasons he'd bought the *Bonus* was to give him a place to spend weekends, out of the reach of the phone or any unexpected visitors.

He'd first met Della Brame outside a café on a snowy day when her car wouldn't start. He'd taken her home on his bike, and they'd begun seeing each other. It had been pretty good for a while—they'd had little in common outside the bedroom, but that had been enough at first. At her insistence, Bey had started squiring her around town to various bars and nightclubs. He'd been bored stiff by the superficiality of the crowd she hung out with, but he'd made good use of the time by filling notebooks with quick character sketches. His waning interest had plunged still further when she'd started asking some pretty pointed questions about what he did for a living.

He'd finally managed to break it off without being too brutal. It didn't pay to antagonize someone in Della's profession. As a socialite turned feature writer for one of the area's largest dailies, she'd built a reputation on detecting all but invisible flaws in the most respectable facades. Bey had worked too hard to perfect his cover to risk blowing it.

He managed to evade Della's repeated invitation by

promising to call when he had more time. And when that day came, he added silently as he replaced the phone in its cradle, he'd be on the other side of the Chesapeake Bay, leaving not so much as a trail of bread crumbs behind him.

Meanwhile, the chili could wait. He had a powerful urge to head for the Eastern Shore again. He'd never had the slightest desire to confide in Della, but Emily was different. He'd have to level with her. In spite of a few notable lapses, he planned to go easy until he could think of some way to let her know about his writing. Still, it wouldn't hurt to drop by and inquire after her injured foot.

Maybe he'd take her something; a woman like Emily deserved to be courted. By all rights, he should be an expert on courtship, but when it came to actual practice, he wasn't so sure he could pull it off. He'd been accused of a lot of things in his lifetime, but never of being courtly. It would have to be something that wouldn't scare her off—no expensive jewelry. And something that would fit in his saddlebag, which meant no flowers.

An irreverent thought occurred to him, and the last of the hardness engendered by Della's phone call disappeared from his face. He wished he had the nerve to present her with a copy of one of his books—say, the latest one, *Reap the Wild Wind.* Not yet, though—not until he felt a hell of a lot more secure with her.

Emily angled the chair so that she could prop her slippered feet on the fire screen. For once, she'd drawn a book she was thoroughly enjoying. The biography of an English archaeologist who'd devoted his life to a study of Mexican prehistory, it covered a fascinating correspondence with a holy man in India that posed some intriguing questions. She'd love to take a course in archaeology someday.

Her storm windows went unhung and her shutters unpainted, but her conscience was clear. It was too cold and damp out there to risk pneumonia, especially when she had a good fire, a good book and a pot of hambone soup on the stove. She'd earned herself a break.

At the rap on the front door, she looked up in exasperation. There'd been a meeting of the board on Thursday night, and Abbie had mentioned dropping by sometime this weekend. But not now, Emily thought plaintively. Dammit, she was in no mood for discouraging news. Eastwood Academy's days were strictly numbered unless the board had found a fairy godmother—they all knew it, but couldn't the official notification wait until Monday? She'd had the devil of a time regaining her peace of mind, and it wasn't fair to have it shattered again so soon.

Resignedly she threw open the door. "Come on in Ab . . . Bey?" Still holding the book with a finger to mark her place, she gazed at the black-clad figure who stood grinning at her. It had started to drizzle, and there was a film of moisture on his leather coat and the helmet he held under one arm.

"Brought you something," he said almost shyly.

"You . . . why . . . hello, Bey," she stammered inanely. Hurriedly she held the door wider. "Come inside. It's turned colder, hasn't it?"

His eyes mocking her confusion, he stepped inside, pulling the door shut after him. From beneath his helmet he produced a small gold-mesh bag filled with foil-wrapped chocolates. "Hope you like candy. I'd have brought flowers, but I didn't think they'd stand the trip."

"Bey, you didn't have to . . ." Breaking off, Emily led him across to the chair before the fire. "Take off your coat, it's wet. Your pants are . . . Oh. They're leather too." She found herself staring at the close-fitting black pants in fascination. "Don't they get hot?"

Oh, Lord, she'd had to ask. Whatever social graces she'd once possessed had long since deserted her.

Peeling off his coat, Bey turned and said with perfect urbanity, "As a matter of fact, they do."

For several moments they simply stared at one another, Emily feeling as if her veins had been pumped full of sweet sparkling wine. She hadn't expected to see him so soon, not after the way they'd parted the weekend before. She'd been so afraid he'd take advantage of her momentary weakness that she'd practically rushed him through the door, coffee and all. And then she'd spent almost the entire week thinking about him.

"How've you been?" he asked. As his smile widened, his eyes seemed to grow more amber than green.

"Just fine, and you?" Oh, lovely, she jeered silently. He'll really be entranced by my scintillating conversation!

"I never got around to showing you that flower, did I?"

Puzzled, she held out her hand for the coat he'd removed. "I'll hang it over a chair until it's dry. You mean the flower you found growing at the Landing?

111

No, you never did. My visit ended sort of abruptly, remember?"

"Ouch. In case you hadn't noticed, there are a few rough edges on my party manners. I'm trying, though —bear with me, will you?"

He did it so easily, deflecting her criticisms so that she wanted to cradle him in her arms and soothe away any pain her barbed words had caused. Men like Bey Jones should be made to wear a warning label: CAUTION; could cause serious weakness in women.

"What did it look like?" she asked, gesturing to the Morris chair and taking a seat on the other side of the room.

He held up a fist and lifted one knuckle above the others. "Sort of like this. It was red—sort of purplish red—and it grew on a vine with beans and lacy leaves."

Emily laughed. "It's a wild sweetpea. I didn't know there were any blooming this late in the season. I used to collect great bunches of them when I was little—I remember I was disappointed that they didn't taste at all sweet."

Bey relaxed against the chintz-covered cushions. The heat from the fireplace had brought a flush to his face after the long, cold ride. "This is nice," he murmured, glancing around the room. "Did I tell you I'm going to have a fireplace?"

"I believe you did happen to mention it once or twice," Emily murmured gently. There—he'd done it again, damn him. It took no more than that oddly disarming candor of his to turn her into pudding. Another man might boast about his yacht or his horse or an expensive sports car, and she'd be completely turned off. Bey mentioned a fireplace and her silly heart went into a tailspin.

"How's the building?" she asked, her voice a shade huskier than usual.

"All framed in, I hope—haven't checked it out yet. I'm on my way now."

"Bey, you're not camping out in this weather?"

"Got a better idea?" The grin widened, its very guilelessness raising her defenses.

"I certainly have. There are plenty of rooms in St. Michaels. You could get a good night's sleep in a motel and come back in the morning. You can't see anything in this rain, anyway."

"It's supposed to clear up before long—clearing and colder, according to the noon report."

She nodded resignedly. If he was going to be huddled up in that flimsy little tent on a rainy night while the temperature dropped down into the twenties, she wouldn't be able to sleep a wink. Dammit, why did he have to do this to her? Here she'd finally managed to put the whole silly affair into perspective; she'd caught up on her paperwork and drawn a really good book for once, and now she wouldn't be able to enjoy it for worrying about him.

"I'll be just fine. My sleeping bag's good down to fifteen degrees, and I've got on wool long johns."

"It's wet out there, Bey. You won't be able to heat water, much less get warm," she said resentfully. Why did he have to come along and ruin her whole weekend?

"I'll drink beer."

"For breakfast? That's disgusting."

His grin never wavered as he picked up the gold-mesh bag from the coffee table and opened it. He peeled one of the chocolates and popped it into his mouth. "No it's not. Goes great with sardines and crackers. Of course, the crackers aren't much good in this kind of weather, but then, you can't have everything."

"*Every*thing! You don't have *any*thing!" she argued indignantly.

"Give me time," he murmured, reaching for another chocolate. "I've got plans to have it all." There was something decidedly disturbing about that voice, nor could she find anything at all reassuring in the way his eyelids drooped lazily over those wickedly gleaming eyes.

"I . . . Do you . . . That is, I've got a pot of soup on the stove. It's late for lunch and early for dinner, but maybe you'd better have something to fortify you before you take off."

The whispering sound of soft leather accompanied his rising. He stood before her, looking disconcertingly masculine as he bit into another chocolate. "Sounds great. I was always a sucker for homemade soup."

She led the way into the kitchen. "It may not be the world's greatest soup, but it certainly beats beer and sardines on a day like this," she said defensively. "Do you mind eating in the kitchen again? My furnace is on the blink and the dining room's on the north side of the house."

"I know you'll find this hard to believe, but I rarely stand on ceremony," he teased, enjoying the way the color came and went under her translucent complexion.

He watched her move around the room, reaching to take down bowls, opening the silverware drawer and then shoving it closed with an unconsciously graceful swing of the hips. That was a nice move. And the way her sweater hugged her breasts when she lifted her arms to the top shelf made his pupils dilate with pleasure. Everything about her was lovely. Why couldn't he have settled for some ordinary woman instead of shooting for the stars? She had everything —looks, intelligence, background, a career and a home of her own.

She was gold, he was dross. What the hell did he have to offer her? Looks? He'd seen better-looking faces at the zoo—behind bars. Intelligence? Okay, he'd grant himself a few points there. He was a little short on formal education, but he'd get by. Background? That was a laugh. His background consisted of a series of foster homes and institutions, plus a rumor that his old man had been a merchant seaman. As for his mother, she was ninety percent imagination and ten percent bad memories. When it came to background, he didn't have a whole lot to offer any woman, much less a woman like Emily McCloud.

He was hungry. Breakfast had been black coffee. After Della's call he'd been too damned anxious to split town to hang around for lunch. "This is purely ambrosial," he murmured, scraping up the last spoonful of the richly flavored soup.

"Purely ambrosial," Emily repeated in awed amusement, reaching for his bowl. "Does that mean you want seconds?"

"Can you spare it?"

She couldn't resist. "You realize you're now back in

my debt. One plate of Stroganoff and two bowls of soup to one and a half of your hotdogs."

Their eyes met in shared laughter that had seemed to spring up from nowhere. Emily marveled at how quickly he could affect her mood. One minute she was wishing she'd never laid eyes on the man, and the next she was wondering how the kitchen could feel so sunny on a cold and rainy afternoon in November.

Bey asked about the book she'd been reading, and eagerly she launched on a summary. "It makes me wish I could take off for Mexico—especially on a day like this."

"You like nonfiction best, then?" he asked idly, rising to pour the coffee she'd made.

"Oh, I like everything if it's well-written."

"That's a pretty broad statement." He sipped the steaming coffee and gazed at her quizzically.

She shrugged. "When I was growing up I read everything, and I *do* mean everything—much to my father's horror."

A slow grin deepened the creases in Bey's weathered cheeks. "And here I thought you'd been so sheltered," he scoffed gently. "What do you mean by everything—girlie magazines? *Popular Mechanics?* Cookbooks? Romances?"

In the living room, the mantel clock chimed the hour and a log settled noisily in the fireplace. Someone rang the doorbell.

"Abbie," Emily muttered, excusing herself and rising reluctantly to answer the door. She was aware of a surge of irritation that had nothing at all to do with the possible bad tidings her friend might be bearing.

"Lord, it's miserable out there," the wiry redhead

declared, shaking the raindrops from her scarf and sniffing appreciatively. "What's cooking? Am I too late or too early?"

"Right on the button. Come on out to the kitchen and have a bowl of soup," Emily invited, bowing to the inevitable. She made the introductions, not missing Abbie's swift look of interest. "Abbie, this is Bey Jones. Bey, Abbie Linga. Abbie's headmistress at the school where I teach."

Abbie fluffed the orange hair that had been flattened by her scarf and treated herself to a thorough survey of the compactly built man in the black leather pants and brown knit shirt.

"Wellwellwell," she drawled, "I'm beginning to see why no one can drag Em away from this rural retreat of hers. And all along I thought she was too busy doing her schoolwork to come out and play." She accepted the bowl of soup Emily served her and proceeded to ignore it. "Do you live around here, Bey? And is your first name Chesapeake, by any chance?"

Emily's head swung from one of them to the other as they settled the matter of Bey's unusual name and his reason for being here. She felt rather like a spectator at a tennis match.

"So—you're going to be neighbors," Abbie murmured, a speculative gleam in her eyes. Emily could have killed her. Evidently all those romances she'd read had softened her brain.

This had gone far enough. "I suppose the news is bad," she broke in, deliberately steering the subject away from the man in her kitchen. "You weren't in your office when I popped in yesterday."

Abbie turned a blank look on her. "Oh . . . that.

Well, I must say, you've at least got some compensation. Now I won't have worry about leaving you here all alone and in despair."

"How long do we have?" Emily asked stoically.

"The rest of this term. We might have lasted out the year except for the asbestos ceilings that have got to come out. It was decided," she announced sarcastically, "to postpone any decision on when to comply until the next term, at which time, of course, Eastwood will have ceased to exist." She planted an elbow on the table and plopped her chin in her palm. "Drat!"

"Seventy-seven years," Emily said morosely. "Do you realize that my grandmother and my mother both graduated from that school?"

"And you."

"And me," Emily echoed, staring absently at a ring of moisture on the polished surface of the table. "I think I'd like a drink."

Bey rose quietly to his feet. "If you'll tell me where and what . . . ?"

"I've only got sherry," she apologized dully. His eyes crinkled into a shadow of a smile, and it irritated her unreasonably. "You think it's funny, my losing a job? I may end up shucking oysters for a living."

His hand rested on her shoulder for a long moment, and Emily found herself wanting nothing so much as to close her mind to her troubles and bury herself in those strong, sheltering arms.

"Matter of fact, one of the reasons I came out here was to sound you out about something," Abbie said briskly.

Bey's smile turned inward as he busied himself with the decanter. He'd known she'd drink sherry. It would be dry, and good, but not too expensive. He served the wine and then swung his chair around to straddle it.

"So sound me out," Emily sighed.

"Ever been to Durham, North Carolina?" Abbie inquired, downing her wine as if it were whiskey.

Emily shook her head, trying to force an interest in what Abbie was saying. Subliminally she was aware of an almost catlike stillness in Bey. He was resting his arms on the back of the chair, his eyes half-closed as he sipped from his wineglass. There was something almost alien about his presence at her table; alien, but somehow . . . right.

"I've been offered a position as headmistress in a small coed school in Durham County. I happen to know that there's an opening in the English department, but the salary won't be too great—at least not for the first year or so. If you're interested, I'm driving down next Friday for an interview."

Bey's eyes opened, and he placed his empty glass on the table. "Let's go in by the fire. Abbie, you can't expect Emily to make a decision like that off the top of her head. Tell me," he said, escorting the small, attractive redhead into the living room and leaving Emily to bring up the rear, "exactly what does a headmistress do? The term conjures up all sorts of interesting possibilities."

Emily's gray eyes grew stony as Abbie bloomed under the attention. Dammit, Abbie had two ex-husbands, a live-in companion, and a decent new job to go to. Did she have to have Bey drooling all over her too?

Somehow she found herself sharing the hard sofa

with Bey while Abbie settled into the Morris chair. Crossing her arms, she leaned back, only to feel Bey's fingers twisting gently in her hair. He was sitting almost three feet away, with one arm stretched out along the back of the sofa, listening to Abbie's job description with every evidence of fascination. Emily tried to pull away from his hand and winced when the fingers tightened in her hair.

"I like your line of thought, Bey. Unfortunately, for the next few weeks I'm going to be busy trying to placate a hundred or so disgruntled parents and help them squeeze their offspring into some other over-crowded, underfinanced institute of learning. Come to think of it, shucking oysters doesn't sound all that bad, Em. Got any good contacts?"

"Next weekend, you say? What time are you planning to leave?" Emily asked, frowning thought-fully.

Bey yanked at her hair again. "Honey, you can't just go dashing off that way. You've got a home here, and a—"

Honey? Emily shot him a repressive look, jerking her hair free of his playful fingers. "And what? How long do you think I can keep this place with no job?"

Abbie reached for the small bag of chocolates Bey had left, helping herself to one of the few that remained. "What about the column?" She turned to Bey. "Emily does this book review every week. She's had this thing going with some reader who took exception to a certain review, and everybody in town's talking about it."

"Oh, Abbie," Emily grumbled.

"Well, they are. Wendell ought to raise your pay for

the increase in sales. He could double his circulation if you'd do just one controversial review a month."

Embarrassed, Emily slanted a glance at Bey. "Abbie's exaggerating. It wasn't controversial. I just didn't like the book."

Bey's eyes probed hers as a smile teased the corners of his mouth. "Didn't like it? Or didn't understand it?"

"It was just a romance, for goodness' sake," she said disparagingly.

Abbie chimed in. "And Emily doesn't care for romances. They're conspiring to undermine the womanhood of America." She peeled another chocolate and slipped it into her mouth, rolling her eyes heavenward. "Look, folks, I hate to eat and run, but duty calls. Why don't you bring a bag on Friday and we'll leave from school. The interview's on Saturday morning at ten, and we can do the town Saturday night and come home Sunday."

Bey stood up. In the cozy cluttered warmth of the small room, he seemed strangely . . . The word "menacing" popped into Emily's head and she shook herself. Black leather pants, a battered face, and the build of a professional athlete did not necessarily add up to menace. She was being fanciful.

"Abbie, I'll let you know by Wednesday," she said hurriedly.

Bey wrapped an arm about her and she shot him a tight-lipped look. "Yeah, she'll let you know, Abbie. Been nice meeting you. Come by again."

The moment the door closed, Emily turned angrily to confront him. "Don't you think it's time you were running along too, Bey? Duck season's started, and you might have to try a couple of places before you find a room." She did her best to ignore her accelerating pulses and the dryness that had her swallowing convulsively. Dammit, why was he crowding her against the door this way?

"I told you I'm not staying in any motel, Emily." He didn't touch her, but the very animal warmth of his body seemed to reach out and surround her, numbing her will to defy him. "I don't mind a little rain," he said, the gravelly texture of his voice more evident than usual under its softness. "I've slept out in worse weather than this without benefit of sleeping bag or tent. I don't melt."

He melted, all right. He melted *her*. Hardening herself against his beguiling spell, she said witheringly, "Well, just so you understand that my hospitality begins and ends in the kitchen."

"You're inviting me to spread my bag on your warm kitchen floor?"

The boyish eagerness was not entirely convincing, not when the virile strength of him, the very scent of him, was undermining her reason. She crossed her arms and did her best to seal herself against his magnetism. "I'm inviting you to leave, Bey. It might strike you as amusing that I've just lost my job, but believe me, I don't find it at all humorous. I've got a lot of serious thinking to do, and I don't need—"

"Humorous?" he broke in. "What the hell gave you the idea I thought it was humorous?"

"Oh, don't try that innocent look on me. I saw you grinning like a Cheshire cat back there in the kitchen. Things may be rosy for you publishers, but let me tell you something, the teaching business has seen better days! I don't find it at all amusing to have to start out at the bottom of the ladder again after all these years."

Without taking a single step, he was suddenly much closer. "Emily, Emily," he whispered, unfolding her arms as easily as if they were made of paper, "you'll be all right. I promise you, you'll be just fine."

7

Helplessly she watched as it began to melt away—the anger, the determination, the firm boundaries she'd set out to define the limits of their relationship. As the spell of him eddied around her, she watched it begin to crumble, undermined as swiftly as sand castles in the tide. Her stricken gaze followed him until the very last moment, seeing the quick softening of his lips, the fierce intensity of heavy-lidded eyes embedded in the hardened planes of his face.

"Bey, please don't?" she pleaded, her voice wavering off into a plaintive question.

It was hopeless. How could she fight against something she wanted beyond all reason? At the first touch of his hard hands on her face, curving along the lines of her jaw, defining the hollow of her cheeks, she surrendered. Her lips parted in the instant before he claimed them. One kiss, she promised herself in desperate resignation. One kiss and then she'd shove him out the door. And heaven help her if she broke that promise.

The darting thrust of his tongue triggered an instant response, and her arms crept around his waist, her hands moving restlessly over the powerful muscles of his back. Her breasts were crushed against him, and she swayed unconsciously, wanting the tactile stimulation of flesh against flesh.

As if sensing her needs, Bey slowly lowered his hands from her face to the hollows of her throat. Then, lifting his mouth to brush kisses over her eyelids, he fitted his palm around the small fullness of her breast, and she sagged against him.

"Oh, God, sweetheart, you don't know how much I've wanted this, wanted you—you just can't know," he whispered hoarsely.

"Bey, this is a mistake," she murmured even as her hands curved over the taut leather-clad muscles of his buttocks. "You've got to go, got to leave me alone." For all the control she had, she might as well be drunk! Somewhere in the back of her mind, a wisp of reason struggled for recognition, but her heedless body was racing at breakneck speed along the path of its own desires.

His hand slipped up under the layers of wool and nylon, his hard palms creating an erotic friction on her sensitive skin. Under her sweater and camisole, she wore nothing. By the time he cupped the lower slopes of her breasts and allowed his thumbs to reach upward, her nipples had already gathered themselves into tight, expectant buds. She felt his quick, surging response as he recognized her state of readiness.

The pale patterned wool of the ancient rug was soft,

warmed by the glow from the fireplace. Bey lowered her to the floor and followed her down. Slipping an arm under her shoulder and another over her hips, he caught her tightly to him.

"Emily, Emily—do you have even the faintest idea what you do to me?" His warm breath stirred her tumbled hair as his tongue found the pink shell of her ear. She shuddered violently. "So perfect, so lovely—I don't deserve you, but God, I want you, sweet Emily—every curve, every swell, every warm, secret place—I want all of you."

Each shimmering word he whispered shot through her body, setting up a rush of tremors as his hands began unbuttoning her sweater. She could only lie there rigid with excitement. Her feet were arched, toes extended downward in the fur-rimmed pink suede slippers. When he slipped the sweater from her arms and tugged it from beneath her, she clung helplessly to the narrow gleam of his eyes, drowning in a cascade of pure sensation.

He knelt beside her, the supple black leather straining across his thighs as he raised his arms and pulled his knit shirt over his head. Her gaze tangled in the dense thicket of surprisingly dark hair on his chest, and her fingers curved unconsciously into her palms. His nipples were flat copper disks, their tiny centers standing proudly alert. Her lips parted in a small groan.

He came down over her slowly, his mouth finding hers in a hungry joining, even as his hands worked at the fastening of her slacks. She could feel the heat spreading through her body, radiating out from an incandescent center that throbbed almost painfully. As his hands slid under her hips to remove her slacks, her legs stiffened again.

He came back to her mouth as though impatient at the momentary delay, alternately suckling and thrusting as his hands began to explore the warm satin of her stomach between filmy white briefs and the lacy camisole. One of his legs moved to cover one of hers, and she marveled with strange detachment at the cool feel of leather against the heated flesh of her thigh.

Bey's lips moved to nuzzle her tumbled hair away from her ear. "I need to see you," he whispered, drawing out the sibilant sound until she arched her back and shuddered in helpless excitement. Quickly he reached under her to slip the flimsy garment over her shoulders.

Somewhere along the way, she'd lost her slippers, and Bey, she noted in vague surprise, had shed his boots. She wanted him to shed everything. She was starving for the sight of him, perishing from a need so elemental that it drove out all else from her mind.

Once more he knelt beside her, his smoldering gaze igniting flames as it ranged over her with lingering deliberation. Bemused, Emily watched the slow journey of his hard, tanned hands as they moved along her milk-white torso. The flat surface of her stomach trembled in anticipation of his touch, and when one of his fingers dipped into her navel, she whimpered, her breath escaping in shuddery little gasps.

In the incredibly erogenous bend of her thigh, he planted a series of moist kisses. And then his tongue began to trace the imperceptible crease. In a rush of exquisite agony, she curled herself around his head.

"Bey, please—I can't stand it," she whimpered.

Lifting his head, he met her beseeching gaze. The planes of his face seemed oddly altered; harsher, yet strangely vulnerable. "Bey . . ." she cried softly, catching at his shoulders to pull him up over her.

"Wait," he grated.

"Ah, please . . ." She read the promise in his eyes, but she needed more than promises. Her body's own sensuality had lain dormant for too long, and now, in awakening, it was threatening to overwhelm her.

Reaching up to the sofa, Bey pulled down a small pillow and slipped it under her hips. "Soon, my sweet lady love," he whispered, his voice harsh with the strain of control. His hand feathered down to her breast to cup, to fondle, to arouse, and the realization that he was trembling too pierced her.

The sweetness that had coiled so tightly in her loins began to unwind, to flow out along her limbs, simmering, shimmering, gathering strength until it encompassed every cell of her body. Half-closed eyes savored the sensuous sight of dark, hair-roughened flesh against creamy smoothness, flaring nostrils drank in the scent of musky masculinity against the familiar fragrance of her body lotion. By the time she felt his tongue circle a throbbing nipple, her eyes were tightly closed and she was breathing in shallow little gulps.

In an involuntary reaction, she drew up her knees. The languorous sweetness penetrated the core of her being, and her thighs stirred in an instinctive urge to part.

Abruptly Bey stood, his hooded gaze never leaving her. She lay vulnerable beneath him as he unzipped the close-fitting leather breeches and stepped out of them. Whatever he wore beneath them came off as well, and Emily found her gaze riveted to his powerful, beautifully masculine body. And in the brief moment before he came down to her, she knew that in spite of all reason, it was far more than the virile young body she wanted. She wanted all of him—for all time.

The words he'd whispered to her flickered in her mind, in echo to her own needs. There'd been no word of love, no hint of commitment. If all the caring was on her side and there was only wanting on his, then this would have to be enough.

Bey was actually trembling with the strength of his desire, and yet even though he must know that her own need was every bit as fierce as his, he held back. With a tenderness she found incredibly moving, he knelt to kiss her thighs apart, murmuring broken words of reassurance. She'd been left in no doubt as to the extent of his expertise, but now he seemed almost hesitant, unsure—not at all like a tough, magnetically attractive man who must have known scores of women.

She ran her hungry hands down his body, encouraging, beseeching, discovering. His flesh was warm and resilient, its texture silken under her sensitive fingertips. As she encountered the rougher terrain where the crisp-soft hair patterned downward, she followed it.

"Emily . . . !" He swore softly as her hands claimed the velvet-sheathed steel of him. She felt a soaring need to give him all the pleasure, to lift him to spinning heights. Instinct as old as womankind guided her until she sensed that he was all but beyond control.

With a rasping oath, Bey lifted her aside. God! And to think he'd once accused her of being incapable of appreciating her own womanhood.

He came into her then, his control completely

shattered by an explosive force that went far beyond the limits of anything he'd ever experienced before. In the wild, swift climb that carried them heedlessly to the sun and then hurled them beyond it, he became a part of her very consciousness, welded physically, mentally, spiritually into a union that had at its center the white heat of a nova star.

Together they drifted downward, clinging, bathed in heated moisture, gasping for breath. All the lights in the universe glowed softly around them, and from a great distance came the sound of ceaselessly drumming rain. They slept.

Sometime during the night, Bey awoke and threw another log on the fire. He prowled the house until he located a blanket, and with a feeling of tenderness that scared the hell out of him, he allowed it to drift down over the woman who slept on the floor, arms and legs sprawled in an unconscious grace that was beauty incarnate.

Fighting down the panic that threatened him, he knelt and slid beneath the blanket, gathering her into his arms again.

A streak of watery sunlight greeted her as Emily opened her eyes. An assortment of unfamiliar impressions rushed in on her. Her bedroom faced northwest; morning sun never found its window. Her bed was hard, but not this hard, and the shoulder her head was resting on was much firmer and warmer than her goose-down pillow.

Her eyes closed against sudden realization. She was in the living room. She was on the floor. They'd made love, and he was still here, and heaven help her, she was in love with him.

It came again, the sound that had dragged her from the depths of sleep. Sitting up, she grabbed the naked shoulder beside her and shook it fiercely.

"Bey! Wake up, dammit—there's someone at the front door!" she whispered furiously.

He was instantly alert, his wits in readiness, his body lagging only slightly behind. It took him less than a second to assimilate the situation. "Tell 'em to wait one minute. I'll scoop up our gear and head for the bathroom while you put on a robe."

Lunging for a slipper, Emily jammed her foot in it, grumbling under her breath. "Any idiot who'd come calling at the crack of dawn on Sunday morning . . . !"

Bey was on his feet, totally unselfconscious in his nakedness. "Honey, dawn cracked quite a few hours ago. Did you invite anyone to Sunday dinner?"

He handed her another slipper and she hopped on one foot while she put it on, casting him a reproachful glance over her shoulder. "Why did you let me sleep so late? Dammit, why did you . . . ?" And then, lifting her head, "Just a minute!" she called out irritably.

When she headed for the bathroom where her robe hung behind the door, Bey was one step behind her, trailing an armload of clothing and bedding, incongruously topped off by a pair of rugged leather boots. "Are you always this delightful in the morning?" he whispered.

"I'm a dragon in the morning! Would you please get dressed and get out of here? And use the back door."

"Don't I even get breakfast?" he asked plaintively.

Whirling around, Emily jerked her white quilted robe together and knotted the sash. "This is *not* a bed-and-breakfast establishment, Bey. Just get out and stay away from me, is that clear?"

They stood in the bathroom doorway, and she turned to confront him, anger hiding the anguish on her pale features. Her eyes dropped, only to encounter a pair of high-arched bare feet, the toes curled against her cold floor. Her gaze traveled up a pair of hairy, muscular legs, to the ludicrous bundle he held against him, and from there it swept out to each of his broad, coppery shoulders. Centering once more on his strong tanned throat, it lifted reluctantly to that battered, impossibly dear face.

He was grinning at her. Hazel eyes glowing like amber, white teeth gleaming in imperfect splendor, he met her stony glare with all the aplomb of fully clothed king of his realm.

The buzzer sounded again, and with an impatient oath Emily shoved past him. "Just be sure you're out of here before I come back," she snarled.

Her scowl gave way to astonishment as she opened the door to see Wendell Twiford. "Good Lord! I mean, good morning, Wendell. What on earth brings you out here at *any* time of day?" At *any* time of day. In spite of their occasional dates, it had been years since Wendell had set foot on her porch.

"I heard the news, of course." He removed his Irish tweed hat and smoothed the surface of his graying hair. "Em, I'm really sorry. I've been meaning to call, but you know how it is—one crisis after another. Say, may I come in? No point in letting all your heat go out the door."

Grudgingly she backed away, allowing him to enter the living room. A swift, apprehensive glance assured her that there was no evidence of her overnight guest in sight. Then, as the sound of the shower registered on her consciousness, she clenched her teeth in impotent fury.

"Well, now, maybe we can put our heads together and come up with something to tide you over until you can get situated again. I knew there was trouble, but I didn't realize how bad things were." His pale eyes reflected a sympathy that she found thoroughly distasteful. "I guess this is why you came to me asking about another column. You should have leveled with me, Em. I'd have found you something—art coverage, maybe. You could cover the Waterfowl Festival exhibit for me. Nancy doesn't have to do it every year."

Another fifteen bucks, she thought rancorously. That would help a lot! The shower was still going. She only hoped that if Wendell noticed the sound he'd put it down to something else. "Look, Wendell, thanks for your concern, but I'm fine." She'd be damned before she'd take his charity. "There'll be severance pay and all that, I suppose—I'm not hurting, honestly."

Wendell sat, after carefully pinching the creases in his dark gray pinstripe. "Tom Brady did a feature for today's edition, file stuff, mostly—brief history, alumnae who've gone on to fame and fortune, old families that have contributed so much—that sort of thing. Your own grandfather posthumously donated a wing, remember?"

The sound of the shower was glaringly absent, and Emily felt a sudden inappropriate surge of recklessness. "Actually, it was a drumstick—the concert shell in the auditorium."

Wendell's lips tightened disapprovingly. "You never change, do you, Em? In a pinch, one can always count on you to say something frivolous."

"It's my pinch, Wendell, and if I want to be frivolous, that's my business."

"I was *trying* to do you a favor," he reminded her witheringly.

"And I appreciate it, Wendell—I do," she assured him, vaguely ashamed of herself for not appreciating it more. On the verge of offering coffee, she thought better of it. "Don't worry about me, Wendell, I'll be just fine. I've already got something lined up."

The look of relief on his narrow patrician face was unmistakable. Oddly enough, Emily appreciated the sense of duty that had prompted his offer far more than the offer itself. It was ironic that the single-minded sense of duty they both possessed had been the very quality that had come between them.

But then, remembering what had happened in that very room only a few hours before, Emily knew that what she'd felt for Wendell had been little more than friendship. Theirs had been that pathetic cliché, a suitable match.

The ominous silence in the back of the house nibbled at her nerves. She stood up, arranging a bright smile on her face. "Wendell, I haven't even had time to dress yet—my brain's still asleep. Why don't I call you in a day or so and we'll work out something about the book reviews. I may be moving out of town after the first of the year."

"Moving! Where? More to the point, why?"

"Why do you think? This place isn't exactly a hotbed of industry."

"Em, you can't leave this place. McClouds are a part of the very backbone of the Eastern Shore." His look of indignation would have been touching if she hadn't been so distracted.

"Look, Wendell . . ." She broke off as Wendell's shocked eyes slid past her. *Oh, no—he wouldn't!* Burying her chin in the high collar of her robe, she closed her eyes and waited.

"Ready, honey?" Bey's voice, ingenuous, cheerful, sounded from the doorway. "What, not even dressed yet? Oops—sorry. Didn't mean to intrude."

If it weren't so embarrassing, it would be funny. Or did she mean that the other way around? Lord, at this point she didn't know what she meant. She was giddy! Lifting her head slightly, she saw Wendell's thin lips open, close, and then open again. He reminded her of something she'd seen at the aquarium.

Bey strode into the room, clad in the leather breeches and boots, with a peach-colored towel draped around his neck. His chin bore a streak of suds, and he was holding her lavender razor in the hand he was extending to Wendell.

"Oops—sorry again," he said cheerfully, shifting it to the other hand.

Somehow, Emily managed to get through the next few minutes without committing mayhem. Her anger soared to such monumental heights that it was utterly impossible to maintain. It became funny. And the more she tried to keep a straight face, the funnier it became. By the time she saw Wendell on his way, no wiser as to just what Bey Jones was doing in her bathroom, shaving with her razor, she was ready to collapse.

"You . . . Damn you, I told you to get out," she sputtered, falling back onto the sofa and covering her face with her hands. She felt the springs yield beside her, smelled the scent of her shampoo. "You used my shampoo," she accused, as if that were the prime offense.

"I had to use something—I've got a tough beard."

The very reasonableness of his explanation set her off again, and she could no longer contain herself. She howled, toppling away from him to lean against the inhospitable arm of the sofa.

She felt the tentative touch of a hand on her thigh. "Emily? Sweetheart, are you all right?"

"Oh, Lord, why didn't you just leave?" she gasped.

"I needed a shower—you needed time to cool off. I had no intention of walking out of here before we'd talked." His voice seemed to gain strength as he spoke. "Look, I don't know who this Twiford guy is to come barging in here the way he did, but he's not good enough for you."

He was still shaken by the depth of the jealousy that had cut through him at the sight of that smooth SOB. He'd never experienced anything faintly like it before. "I know his type," he jeered. "The veneer goes all the way through—no blood, no guts."

Sobering, Emily wiped her eyes. "And you'd be the expert on blood and guts, of course." She turned in time to see the swift darkening of his eyes, but then it was gone, so quickly she thought she must have imagined it.

There was a stillness about him that disturbed her. His voice, when it came, was unusually quiet. "Yeah, I suppose I am. But don't make the mistake of thinking that's all I'm an expert on, Emily."

And then, with a mercurial shift of mood that easily matched her own, he said, "Run put on something warm—a pair of rubber boots if you've got 'em—and let's go see my house. Who knows, I might even have the hearth of my fireplace by now."

"I haven't even had coffee yet," she wailed, amazed at how much his suggestion appealed to her.

"You get dressed while I make it, okay? If you're a good girl, I'll even fix breakfast."

"I must have a death wish," she muttered, shaking her head. "Five minutes, and it had better be good."

"Where is it?" she asked some ten minutes later. Five minutes to shower, five to pull on her old flannels, the violet cashmere, and step into a pair of wool socks. She was starving!

"Found your thermos." He tapped the stainless-steel container. "The rest is in the bag." He indicated a brown paper bag on the table. "Now go finish getting dressed. Jump into your boots and get a coat on. You need a hat, too—your hair's wet."

"Can this be the same Emily McCloud I've known for thirty-seven years, calmly allowing some strange man to order her around in her own home?" She retrieved her vinyl Wellingtons from the utility room and tugged them on.

"Quit harping on your age," Bey growled playfully,

"and do as I say, or some strange man might help you get *undressed*."

I'm a classic fool, she told herself, fitting a lopsided orange crocheted hat over her thick, damp hair. I don't know a single thing about him except that he's five years my junior, a rough, tough biker who *claims* to have something to do with a respectable business—and heaven help me, I think I love the man.

Steam rose from the carpet of wet leaves as the sun's rays beat down on the sodden ground. Naked tree trunks glistened blackly, and here and there a stubborn oak clung proudly to its autumn coat of color.

"Your boots are going to be ruined, you know," Emily remarked smugly as her own waterproof ones began to collect a rim of dun-colored mud.

"Hate to disappoint you, honey, but they've got enough neat's-foot oil on 'em to walk on water."

She glanced pointedly at the muddy engineer's boots. "I always knew you had feet of clay."

He swatted her on the backside with the paper bag. "Does that mean you think I'm an idol?"

"Hardly. Speaking of idol—not the clay-footed variety—what do you do with yourself when you're not here? What sort of things do you publish?"

"My darlingest Emily, I make it a policy never to discuss work before breakfast."

The door was closed so softly that she could only accept the polite rebuff. Besides, under the magical spell of the freshly washed forest, she felt incredibly invigorated, completely alive. She swung along beside him, her long-legged stride challenging his to keep up with her.

He did so easily. Carrying the brown bag and the

thermos of coffee, he moved with a strong graceful-ness that alone set him apart from any man she'd ever met. The word "Indian" came to mind, but if there was a vestige of Indian blood in him, it was well disguised. His name was Welsh, he had the tenacity of the Scots, the silver tongue of the Irish, and Lord knows *what* else from *where* else.

"Where'd you come from, Bey? I mean your family?" She had a bit of the Scots tenacity her-self.

"Say, here's that vine I was telling you about," he exclaimed, pointing with the thermos to a wither-ing tangle of pale green. "Nothing but beans on it now."

She gave up. If he wanted to tell her, he would. If he didn't, nothing short of thumbscrews would pry it out of him. An irreverent grin crinkled her eyes. Come to think of it, in a case of thumbscrews versus Bey Jones, she'd bet on Bey.

He held aside a long bramble cane for her to pass, and then they paused to admire the delicate frosting of pale blue that preceded its seasonal demise. "I'm going to know the name of everything that grows in this land, every bird, every insect, every—"

"Rock?" she ventured, melting all over again at his undisguised enthusiasm. Among the more sophisti-cated men she'd known all her life, enthusiasm was considered gauche unless it was for sports, yachts, or certain prestige automobiles.

"I read a book on rocks once—igneous and sedi-mentary rocks, schists and gneisses and some I can't even pronounce."

"I know granite and quartz. That's about the extent of my geological knowledge," Emily admitted. "What

I'd really like to delve into is archaeology. Geology would probably be a help there."

"Do you know about birds?" he asked eagerly as they neared the construction site.

"By sight, most of them. By song, not that many," she admitted.

"I've got a book. I've got a lot of books. The minute this place is closed in, I'm going to start moving in. You can help me set up my library, all right?"

At the sight of the insulated siding and the newly sheathed roof, they both forgot about books. Emily moved forward and then stopped to wait for Bey, who was standing as though frozen, his expression strangely vulnerable. It struck her that she'd seen a similar look on his face just before he'd made love to her.

Shaken, she moved on to the edge of the clearing and waited until he joined her. A feeling not unlike jealousy twisted inside her as she watched the reverent way he approached the structure. She might as well not have been there for all the attention he paid her, and it hurt. It hurt like the very devil. It also puzzled her.

It was only a house, and not even a very large house, at that. She hadn't the faintest conception of square footage, but it couldn't be too much larger than her own place. Through the large opening that would be a front door, she could see the corner of a raised hearth. Bey leapt agilely up through one of the openings and stood, his back to her as he gazed downward.

After a long while, he turned. Emily, leaning against a stack of fragrant wet lumber, hadn't moved at all.

"Shall we have our breakfast in my kitchen?" he asked.

A smile that reminded her of sunshine after rain broke across his face, and she felt her eyes filming over in an absurd rush of emotion.

Dammit, if this was what being in love was going to do to her, she wouldn't last out the month!

8

꩜

Swearing impatiently, Bey ripped the page from the typewriter, wadded it into a ball and tossed it to the floor with the others. The area surrounding his desk was beginning to resemble a snowball factory. He shoved back his chair and stood up, eyeing the array of half-empty coffee cups and cracker crumbs. He'd stayed awake by drinking gallons of black coffee. When he'd run out of food, he'd gone to the nearest vending machine and bought a dozen packs of cheese crackers.

He *had* to get this thing into the hands of his agent, and this time, dammit, he was going to accept the multi-book contract his publisher had been trying to make him sign since his second book.

Up until now he'd been content to take it one step at a time, venturing only what he could afford to lose. One book at a time—he could handle that. Until now, the money hadn't been all that important—it had never seemed quite real, anyhow, since it had gone directly from his agent to his accountant. He'd subsisted on the small amount of investment income that hadn't been plowed back into his portfolio.

The real satisfaction had come from knowing that he was a damned good writer who got better with each book. But satisfaction was no longer enough. The cards were stacked too heavily against him; he'd need every advantage he could get if he was going to win her.

On Wednesday he called his agent, Frank Satchell. Half an hour later he was on his way to the airport. A shuttle would put him into Kennedy before noon. After that it depended on how fast Frank could push things through for him. Whatever happened, he intended to be back on the Eastern Shore come the weekend.

It had been a while since he'd suffered a suit and tie, but if it would move things along at a faster pace, then it was worth it. He'd long since learned the advantage of protective coloration, and that went for Madison Avenue as well as the bay country. Where he was going, the brothers Brooks would open more doors than Levi Strauss.

As a protective measure against the cattle-car ambience of the shuttle, he turned his thoughts inward to that last frustrating few minutes with Emily.

They'd sat on the floor eating peanut-butter sandwiches and tollhouse cookies, washing it down with the coffee from the thermos. She'd chided him about his atrocious taste in foods, and he'd rambled on about the house. To his delight, she hadn't seemed bored. If he hadn't had the house to talk about, he'd have made an even bigger fool of himself. It had been all he could do to keep his hands off her, but he'd known damned well that if he touched her, it would start up all over again. He wanted her, God knows, but he wanted *all* of her—for keeps. And he had a hell of a lot of groundwork to lay before he could ask her to marry him.

They'd talked about heating systems. They'd talked about floor finishes and other prosaic things that hadn't interested him one damned bit at the moment. They'd talked about fireplaces and the best woods to burn. With that little frown of hers that made her look so endearingly studious, she'd told him he should start cutting and drying his firewood now for the following year.

"If you want to keep your chimney clean, Bey, you should really dry your wood for at least a year." Her eyes had looked everywhere except at him, and he'd wondered if she was remembering the night before, in front of her fireplace.

"I'll raid your woodpile and then you can share my hearth," he'd suggested, only half-teasing.

And then she'd told him he could have all her wood since she probably wouldn't be here, and he'd panicked.

"What do you mean, you won't be here? Of course you'll be here." He'd stood up, glowering down at her as he tried to hide his dismay, and when she'd refused even to look at him, he'd dropped to his knees, grabbing her and pulling her against him.

"Don't tell me that, Emily—you're not going anywhere, and you know it."

She was stiff as a poker in his arms, and he cursed

his own ineptitude. He *knew* better. Dammit, she was the sort of heroine he'd written about over and over. He knew better than to try to force his will on her.

"Emily, Emily, listen to me," he'd whispered hoarsely, and then he'd kissed her. All the pent-up love in him had come welling up then, from a source that went deep into his past, a source that had never been tapped before.

The fine, fragile strength of her had lain still against him while he'd ravaged her mouth like some wild brute. She hadn't resisted, but she hadn't responded, either. After a while he'd made himself release her, and she'd brushed herself off as if she'd rubbed up against something unclean. It had almost killed him.

"Emily, I'm sorry," he'd groaned. "Dammit, you know I wouldn't hurt you for the world." He'd wanted so desperately to tell her how much he loved her, but the words that arose to his throat had lodged there to choke him.

"Do I?" she'd asked distantly, reaching for her coat. "You'll understand if I eat and run—I have a lot to get done if I'm going away next weekend."

"Emily!"

She'd refused to look at him as she went about gathering the rest of her belongings—her thermos, the crocheted hat she'd pulled off to allow the sun to dry her hair. As if they'd been discussing the autumn colors, she'd said, "I understand Durham's lovely. I'll probably miss the bay, though."

He'd been scared as hell and it had come across as anger. "What do you mean, you'll miss the bay? You can't leave here!"

She'd turned to face him then, spine straight,

eyebrows arching slightly over her clear gray eyes. She'd given him a look that would have withered steel. "I beg your pardon?"

Helplessly he'd heard himself say, "You can't go now, Emily. What about us?"

"Us? As in you and me?" She'd never looked more desirable, and he'd never felt more miserable.

"What about your house? You can't just walk out and leave a house like that shut up over the winter."

She'd shrugged carelessly. "I'll sell it."

"Just like that, huh? Unload the whole damned works on some damned fool whim! Who the hell's going to oblige you by taking it off your hands, busted furnace, peeling paint, termites and all?"

"Did anyone ever tell you you have a foul vocabulary? You are, and I do *not* have termites."

"The hell with my vocabulary! Lady, if I'm your only hope, you're in bad shape."

That had been three days ago. She'd walked away, and he'd stood there and watched her, angry, hurting and scared as hell. He'd aged ten years since then. He'd written and rewritten the scenario, but the ending was always the same. On paper, it was so easy—but then, his heroes were all tall, handsome, successful dudes who managed to combine savvy with savoire faire.

Oh, he could write 'em, all right, but when it came right down to it, he couldn't speak the lines to save himself.

New York still smelled the same. Time to pull himself together and get his mind on business. He handed over a twenty and a five and was gone before the cab pulled away from the curb. Swearing softly under his breath, he tried once more to put the matter of Emily

McCloud out of his mind—or at least to the back of it. Right now he had a contract to consider, but after that, he was going to go back there and make her listen to him while he laid his cards on the table—such as they were.

He'd never kidded himself about his looks; not even his mother could have loved him. He was quite literally a bastard. He had no fancy degrees, no illustrious ancestors—that he knew of—and he made his living producing something she professed to despise.

Emily, on the other hand, was everything he was not. She had more class in her little finger than any woman he'd ever met, but in spite of all her breeding, her old-family, old-money background, she *needed* him. She'd come alive before his very eyes. In fact, it was just now sinking in that she'd been more surprised than he had at the depth of her passion.

Emily handed back the essays that had been done for a project that would never get off the ground. At least not in this school. "I'd suggest you save these," she'd told her class. "They're excellent, on the whole, and someday you may want to polish them and submit them to . . ." To whom? They'd be split up, transferring to half a dozen other schools in all probability. "To the historical society, or the *Talbot Light*. Maybe someone will want to go on with our project."

Knowing their days together were now numbered, the girls had seemed to mature overnight. Emily knew she'd miss them. It no longer seemed important that they spent more time reading romances than they did early-twentieth-century poets. At least they read.

The Waterfowl Festival she'd agreed to cover would mean she couldn't go with Abbie to Durham. Instead, she'd arranged to get off two days the following week and drive down alone. Ironically, she needed the time to think. Until now she'd deliberately crammed every waking hour with activities just so she couldn't think, but it wouldn't go away. She'd put away her ladder and thought of him—she'd used her lavender-handled razor and thought of him again. He was *haunting* her!

Like a fool, she'd waited that day for some sign that what had happened between them had meant something to him—that *she* meant something to him. She'd promised herself she'd stay cool and let him make the next move. Instead, he'd sat there going on and on about his blasted house as if it were Buckingham Palace. When he'd shown no sign of discussing anything more personal than the view from his bathroom windows, she'd started asking a few pointed questions about his personal life.

She'd made a mess of everything, but dammit, how could she trust a man who wouldn't even answer the simplest questions about himself? It was as if he didn't trust her. And if he didn't trust her, then he couldn't love her. And if he didn't love her, then there was no future in seeing him again. She'd practically run away to keep him from the satisfaction of seeing her cry.

After school she dropped by the morgue and read the past coverage of the annual Waterfowl Festival. Tomorrow she'd take her lunch hour and go by the Mayor and Council Building to look over the permanent exhibit again. She'd seen the exhibit before, of course. No one living near Easton could avoid it, when practically every store window in the county was decorated around the same theme.

There was a florist's box on her porch. With a rush of emotions that veered radically from hope to anger and back again, she carried it inside and switched on the overhead light. Deliberately she placed the long gray box on the table while she removed her coat and hung it in the closet. Then she took time to light the fire. The box teased her silently while she changed into her slippers, but she refused to give in to the flurry of hope that had sprung up inside her.

With the fire crackling noisily as it blazed up, she settled onto the Morris chair, picking up the box and fingering the small envelope bearing her name. Could it be from Bey? He hardly seemed the type to send flowers, but then, he had brought her candy. And then proceeded to devour it. Between him and Abbie, she hadn't even had a taste.

On the other hand, he'd hardly be sending her flowers after the cool way they'd parted. She'd half-expected him to come by again, or at least to call. Dammit, she didn't even know where to reach him—on the off-chance that she ever needed to get in touch with him.

Impatiently she ripped the gold cord from the box and threw the lid aside. If it was another dutiful sympathy offering from Wendell, she'd burn it.

Roses. Neither pink, nor white, nor yellow, but a subtle blend of all three colors, they were dewy and exquisite. The perfume drifted up to her nostrils from the bed of green waxed paper as she opened the small envelope.

"They make no pretense, these beautiful flowers, of

being beautiful for my sake, of bearing honey for me; in short, there does not seem to be any kind of relationship understood between us, and yet . . ."

It was signed B.J., with a little help from Richard Jefferies.

Breathing in the spicy essence of the roses, she read the words over and over, always coming back to the ambiguous ending, " . . . and yet . . ."

"B.J.," she murmured, frowning. She'd been stumbling over those initials ever since she'd reviewed that Bonnie Jericho book.

At least she seemed to have heard the last of one of her B.J.'s. There had been no more letters to the editor from the disgruntled romance reader—or writer, if that were the case.

Which left Bey. And since she didn't imagine that the flowers had come from either Miss Jericho or her anonymous defender, they must have come from Bey. As what? An apology? Somehow, it didn't seem quite his style, quoting obscure writers. But then, sending an expensive bouquet hardly seemed his style, either—or did it?

Burying her face in the cool, sweet spiciness, she admitted that, yes, she could easily imagine Bey sending flowers. In spite of his tough appearance, there was something incongruously tender about him, something that had reached out to her in a way that no other man had done in all her life.

She shoved the roses aside impatiently. Dammit, why did he have to drag it out with flowers? How could she start getting over him if he persisted in making these foolish romantic gestures?

* * *

Emily had followed the flying-goose signs painted on the sidewalks until her feet began to protest, and then she'd taken the free shuttle. She'd saved the Gold Room, where the most expensive things were shown, until last, knowing that the work there would blind her to some of the lesser works in other buildings. She was a sucker for a fine painting; last year she'd almost succumbed to a Bob Dance shorescape. Luckily someone else had beat her to it—she'd have had to sell her soul to buy it.

Foot-weary, but with a glow of pleasure lighting her face, she wandered back and forth, studying the various works on display. Her notebook was already scribbled full, the winners in the various categories duly noted.

"How long do you suppose it took to do that one? Every feather's perfect."

Emily turned to see a strikingly attractive woman examining a finely detailed study of a pair of pintails. "Longer than it took the ducks to grow them, I suspect. Did you see the Joe Seme over there?"

"The one by the door? I'm coveting like crazy, can't you tell? Della Brame, Baltimore Sentinel. You know, I'd expected to be pretty bored by all this stuff, but it's really impressive. Have you covered it before?"

"Only unofficially. You can't live around here and escape it." Emily introduced herself and explained, "I'm not really a reporter, I'm only subbing for the woman who usually covers the art news. All I do is a weekly column of book reviews."

The small green-eyed blonde glanced at the notebook, identical to her own, and shrugged. "We all start somewhere. I got my start covering a crab cook-off when the food editor came down with ptomaine. My last piece was a cover story in the Sunday supplement —estuarine pollution."

"You're that Brame, then." Emily tucked her notebook into her purse and turned to study the other reporter. "I read the estuary thing. You must have stepped on a few toes in that one."

"I sincerely hope so. I'm planning a doozy of a follow-up if things fall out the way I expect them to. Say, are you hungry? I'm starved, but I hate like sin to eat alone. Is there someplace where we could actually sit down?"

Charmed by the easy friendliness from a bona fide reporter, Emily smiled ruefully. "You do understand that the population around here more than triples for this thing, don't you? We can try, though. What do you like, clam chowder? Crab sandwich? Oysters on the half shell?"

She turned toward the door and froze in her crepe-soled tracks. Before she could react to the sight of Bey's leather-coated figure blocking traffic just inside the door, Della darted forward.

"Beyard! What are you doing here? Why didn't you let me know you were coming? We could have come together."

Standing stock-still, Emily met Bey's gaze, both of them ignoring the effervescent woman who was rapidly closing in on him. At the last possible moment, Bey dragged his eyes away from Emily's and turned toward Della.

Of all the lousy breaks. Here he'd taken time only to change his clothes after getting in from New York, just so he could start patching things up again, and now *this* had to happen. It was a thousand-to-one shot, finding her elbow to elbow with Della. He'd had the devil's own time finding her at all. As a last resort he'd tried the paper, and Twiford had told him she was covering this thing. He'd spent the morning accosting every tall, slender brown-haired woman in sight.

"Don't I get a kissy-kissy?" Della clasped her hands behind his neck, and Bey reddened painfully. "I heard you'd bought some property in this neighborhood, Bey," she purred, ruffling the hair at the back of his head, "but I didn't expect to run into you here."

"No . . . I . . . that is, yes. Della, do you mind? This is a public place." Bey unfolded her arms from around his neck, his color deepening, to her obvious amusement.

"Oh, my, aren't we being proper, though—as if you cared one whit for public opinion."

Shooting a swift, agonized glance at where Emily stood rooted, Bey swore under his breath. He resisted the impulse to burst into a spate of explanations, and finally his momentary paralysis was broken by the ruthless elbow of a white-haired woman whose way he was blocking.

"Emily," he said tentatively, ignoring Della to push his way through the crowded room. Halfway there, he watched with a sinking feeling as her chin lifted and the shutters dropped over her eyes. Had he imagined it, or had she looked as stricken as he felt?

"Hello, Bey," Emily said huskily, meeting his eyes now unflinchingly. "Are you enjoying the exhibit? It's a good one this year. Have you seen the—"

"You two know each other?" Della had followed him across the room, and now she looked from one to the other of them, her eyes narrowing on a glint of speculation.

"We're neighbors—sort of," Emily murmured, wondering how to disengage herself from the embarrassing situation. She was finally beginning to understand why Bey was so reticent about his life when he wasn't with her.

"Della, it was good to see you," Bey growled dismissingly. "Now, if you'll excuse us?"

The petite reporter insinuated herself between the pair of them, tucking her arm through Bey's. "Not on your life, sweetie pie. I told you I heard you'd bought some land around here, but that's not *all* I heard. Remember that conference I covered in Washington last June? Well, just last week I ran into one of the agents I'd met there, and guess what she told me? There's a rumor going around about this certain romance writer—you know the one—top of the best-seller list five out of five times? It seems she's something of a mystery, shuns all publicity. Nobody's seen her, nobody knows if she's really a conglomerate of editors or a soap opera star, or what. One of the men in the sports department swears Bonnie Jericho's a pen name for Howard Cosell."

Della's green eyes glittered with secret amusement, and Bey felt the cold sweat breaking out on his back. "So?" he said with admirable coolness.

"Soooo, her frustrated fans are getting pretty steamed about all this secrecy—no autographs, no lurid, detailed biographies. So I intend to do something about it. This agent I was telling you about lunches with Jericho's agent's wife, and over drinks one day . . . well, I'll save the best part until later."

She smiled up into his face with the look of a slightly tarnished angel. "Wanna buy me lunch, sweetie pie?"

The last vestige of color faded from Bey's face. His cheekbones could not have been more sharply defined if they'd been carved from granite as the noise of the enthusiastic crowd came and went in his ears like the roar of a distant plane. "Della . . . dammit, let's get out of here," he growled. Grabbing her slender arm, he wheeled her away, leaving Emily standing there like a pillar of salt.

So much for that tantalizing half-promise: ". . . and yet . . ." Hours later, Emily stared at the wilting roses through burning, reddened eyes. She should have put them in a cooler room, she supposed. Here in the living room, with the dry heat from the fireplace, they wouldn't last three days.

Which was only fitting, she told herself bitterly. Her brief love affair had hardly lasted as long.

On an impulse born of desperation, she dialed the number of the St. Thomas Aquinas Latin Day School in Durham. With any luck, she could change her appointment to an early-Monday-morning one and be back home the same day. If only she'd turned down the Waterfowl assignment and gone with Abbie in the first place, none of this would have happened. She could have gone on living in fool's paradise for a little while longer.

A few minutes later she hung up the phone with a smile of grim triumph. She had an appointment for nine-forty-five on Monday morning. And there was no reason whatsoever that she had to wait around here until the following day. An overnight bag to pack, a call to Wendell in case anyone needed to get in touch with her—the girls would know to call him if they couldn't reach her here, not that they ever called anymore.

Somewhere, she had a résumé—a dozen years out of date, but then, nothing of note had happened to her in all those years. Not until recently, that is, and that would hardly be of any interest to a prospective employer.

By three o'clock she was on her way, having stopped by Bob's place to fill up and have him check under the hood.

"Off for the weekend, Miz McCloud?" he'd asked, wiping a dipstick on a filthy cloth before ramming it home. "Gettin' a late start, ain't ye?"

"Better late than never," Emily acknowledged, shoving aside the bag of review books she'd thrown in at the last minute to unearth her purse.

Wendell would have jeered at her for that one. He'd always pounced on every cliché she uttered, and under pressure, she always managed to utter plenty of them.

Traffic was unusually bad, and she was glad to clear town and head south on Route 50. She'd go down the east side of the bay and come back along the west. Lord knows, she needed a vacation, and she had a day to spare. She switched on the radio to a top-twenty program, taking perverse pleasure in listening to music she abhorred. At least it was far less painful than her thoughts would have been.

Bey pounded on the front door one more time before leaping off the side of the porch and stalking around to the back again. Her car wasn't here. He was dead certain she wasn't either, but he rattled the back door, anyway. Dammit, she couldn't just go off this way. Sooner or later she had to come home, and when she did, he was going to be waiting for her. He'd got rid of Della by promising her an exclusive interview; the next thing he had to do was to explain to Emily.

He should have known it couldn't last forever. The spotlight on the romance industry was no longer as bright as it had been during the big boom, but the very fact that he'd kept a low profile—or rather no profile at all—had been enough to awaken the hunting instincts of a woman like Della. He should have hired himself a stand-in.

Dammit, why now? With every single thing he cared about on the line, he had to stop and placate that ambitious little ferret! A chance meeting, a slip of the tongue over drinks, and that steel-trap mind of hers had done the rest.

In reluctant admiration, he swore softly. He'd seen her go after a highly placed clergyman on nothing more than a standing order of roses—the man's wife was allergic to them, but his mistress, who happened to be the wife of a prominent politician, suffered no such affliction.

The initials hadn't been much to go on, but with that computer brain of hers, Della was too damned good at adding up just such insignificant details. He'd once made the mistake of siding with a panel of romance writers pitted against their detractors on a late-night TV show they'd been watching. His first mistake had been taking her home with him. He'd put away his portable, but he'd forgotten the bookcase. How many men owned a complete set of Jericho novels?

He pounded on the door again. Shading his eyes, he peered through the window into the shadowy kitchen, conscious of a small feeling of reprieve. It wasn't going to be easy. She'd either blister him with scorn, or she'd laugh, and at this point, he didn't know which he feared more.

9

It had to be deliberate. It had to be Wendell's idea of a joke. Three romances—never mind that one of them was historical, one a romantic suspense, and one a two-inch-thick contemporary with a quarter-million-dollar ad campaign already in progress.

"I'll kill him for this," she muttered, glaring down at the three paperback books. No wonder he'd put them in a bag before handing them over. She'd been in too big a hurry at the time to do more than grab and run, but now that she thought of it, there might have been a glint of amusement behind those dark-rimmed glasses. The minute her back was turned, he'd probably started snickering, anticipating her reaction.

Well, if the managing editor thought he was going to trick her into another circulation-building wrangle like the one with B.J., he was in for a long, dry wait, Emily thought rancorously, stabbing the TV switch beside the bed.

She scowled unseeingly at a parade of screeching cars until one of them flipped over and exploded. Then she switched it off again. Her gaze slid to the three books lying beside her on the bed. Regardless of the category, their glossy covers were remarkably similar: low-cut gowns that failed to disguise what they barely covered, anguished expressions that represented either the throes of passion or acute indigestion, boringly handsome men with windblown forelocks and glowering eyes. And the hands . . .

Bey's hands were as square and tanned, and certainly stronger than those of any paperback hero. Against the pale skin of her breasts, they'd looked . . . With a groan, Emily shut her eyes in a vain effort to block out the memory.

Another mental picture drifted into focus: Bey and herself in the classic book-cover pose—Bey, with that crooked grin on his battered face, his wide shoulders covered in black leather, and his denim-clad thighs braced in that aggressively masculine stance that was so characteristic of him. And of course, our heroine, stunning in threadbare lavender cashmere and baggy gray flannel slacks to match her gray-flannel eyes.

How wonderfully romantic. And instead of a castle in the background, there'd be an unfinished house surrounded by dun-colored mud. Instead of a caparisoned stallion prancing restlessly behind the enraptured pair, there'd be a muddy motorcycle, its saddlebags full of camping gear and junk food.

After a long day fraught with too many emotional blows, it was just too much. Emily's lips trembled dangerously, and then she was gasping with laughter. Tears streamed down her cheeks, and after a while, when the laughter turned into sobs, she rolled over and smothered her face in the pillow. In the impersonal shelter of a motel in Chincoteague, Virginia, she cried until her chest ached, her throat was raw, and her eyes were swollen half-shut.

And then she got up and marched to the bathroom, where she splashed handfuls of cold water on her face, liberally soaking the front of her tailored white pajamas in the process. After blowing her nose, she stalked back into the bedroom and reached for the romance with the lusty blond hero on the cover.

Bey camped on the doorstep of the small frame house until the first stars began to show. Waiting was cold business with the temperature already plunging toward a predicted low of twenty-two degrees Fahrenheit. Just before full dark, he strode out to where he'd parked the bike. After scanning the empty road that branched off Route 33 to run out onto the peninsula, he unpacked his sleeping bag and rummaged through the carrier for something to eat. The single can of beer and a half a bag of marshmallows he found wasn't much, but it was better than nothing. Time for steak and brandy when he had something to celebrate.

By the time the moon cleared the opposite shore, Bey had accepted the fact that she was trying to avoid him—and doing a damned fine job of it, too, he swore feelingly. By the time it was directly overhead, he was scared stiff. Pacing the small front porch, he told himself that anything could have happened to her. She could have had an accident. With all the creeks and ditches around here, she could be trapped in her car, slowly freezing to death as the cold, brackish water crept up over her still body.

"Christ!" Closing his eyes against the work of his vivid imagination, he smacked a fist into his palm in a desperate repudiation of his worst fears. She could be lying unconscious in a hospital bed for all he knew.

"Oh, Christ," he uttered in a broken voice. Formal religion had never been a part of his life, but there'd been a few times, times when he'd been completely helpless . . . It was as though his consciousness went into a sort of automatic overdrive. If that was man's spiritual self coming to the surface—if that was what religion was—then so be it.

Expelling a deep, shuddering breath, he considered the situation calmly. She was probably just out with Twiford. He'd called several times after he'd raced back here and found her missing. He'd gone back to town, searching every parking lot, every side street, for a glimpse of her car, and then he'd started calling around. The school, the newspaper—both closed. No answer at Abigail Linga's address in Oxford. Same response at Twiford's home number.

There was something going on between Emily and Twiford. He didn't know quite what it was, but it was a damned sight more than any simple business relationship. He called her Em, which was a desecration of a beautiful name.

Slamming a fist into his palm again, Bey groaned. He could handle almost anything except the agony of not knowing. If she was all right . . . *God, let her be all right!* If she was all right, then he'd leave her alone. He'd speak his piece and then he'd go—which would mean selling the Landing. If he couldn't have her, then he sure as hell didn't want any reminders.

The thought of chucking the whole damned works, the property he'd coveted for so long, the house that was to be his first bona fide home, left him curiously unmoved. Nothing mattered except that Emily was safe.

God knows, if she never gave him so much as another word, she'd have already given him more than any other woman had. Every love story he wrote from now on would be dedicated to her. The miracle was that he'd managed to write one at all. How could he have imagined that love would be like this—a constant heat simmering through his body, an all-consuming fire in his brain, an aching void in his gut whenever he was apart from her?

If she turned him away, he'd have to sell out. He wouldn't be writing anything for a long, long time. Could a heap of ashes string a hundred thousand words together in any cohesive pattern? It had all been a fluke, anyhow. He'd probably hit the road again.

He was awake before daylight on Sunday morning. One look was all it took to tell him that her car was still absent from its usual place. The house was as cold and dark and empty as it had been when he'd finally crawled into his bag and slept in front of her doorway.

Gambling that she wouldn't turn up before noon, having been gone this long, Bey jogged through the woods to water's edge for a brief revitalization, and then he headed for St. Michaels and a decent meal. Seemed that worrying burned considerable calories. He was famished.

By the time he returned to his vigil after an enormous breakfast, he felt somewhat better able to sort things out. He'd been plain stupid to allow Della to stampede him that way. When she'd started dropping ten-pound hints, he'd panicked. His only thought was to get her out of there before she blew his cover to Emily. He should have handled it better, but he'd been taken off guard.

A lot of things had taken him off guard lately, he admitted wryly. It was downright scary to realize just how vulnerable a guy became when he found a woman who meant more to him than life itself.

By eleven o'clock on Sunday night, he was ready to go to the police. Leaving his sleeping bag on her porch, he rode into St. Michaels and located a public phone. There was a string of emergency numbers; he'd call 'em all, from the local cops to the state police, to the hospital, the county sheriff, and even the coast guard.

But first he'd try Twiford again. Just reading those emergency numbers made him break out in a cold sweat. He wasn't sure his fingers were up to the job of dialing them.

A few minutes later he hung up, torn between frustration and relief. Durham. It was so damned obvious he must have been blind not to have figured it out. She'd been planning the trip anyhow, and she'd wanted to get away from him. When Della had thrown herself at him, he'd still been staring at Emily. He'd seen the look on her face, as if he'd just struck her. She'd covered it almost immediately—credit her breeding for carrying it off in royal tradition, but she'd been hurt and puzzled.

And if she'd been hurt, Bey told himself with a cautious return of confidence, then it must mean that she cared at least a little. Under those circumstances, a woman didn't look at a man in that stricken way unless she was feeling *something*. And it wasn't disgust he'd seen staring back at him from those clear gray eyes.

Straddling the bike, Bey zipped up his jacket and flexed his frozen fingers. All he had to do now was be there when she got home. She was due at school Tuesday morning, which meant she'd try to get back as early tomorrow as possible. Five . . . six—seven at the latest. Between now and then, he'd work out a plan of attack.

Trouble was, she might not even realize she cared for him, in which case it was up to him to convince her. Words or action—he wasn't sure which would be the most effective. It would depend on his state of mind when she finally showed up. If he was in the same mental state he'd been in for most of the weekend, then words might have to wait.

Emily got as far as Edgewater before her battery went. She'd braked for a dog just south of the bridge, and the engine had stalled. With traffic piling up behind her, she'd ground frantically on the starter, to no avail. Click-click, and that was it. A truck driver had pushed her car off to one side and then given her a lift to the nearest service station.

Some two hours and fifty-three dollars later, she crossed the bay bridge, hungry, angry and curiously unable to focus her mind on any of the myriad problems besetting her. St. Tommy's, as the school was known locally, had made a favorable impression;

the two members of the board who had interviewed her, equally favorable. An older school, although not quite as old as Eastwood, it had been closed for a year for expansion and a major overhaul. It would be almost like going into a brand-new school.

They'd liked her—Emily was reasonably certain of that. Abbie had told them something of the special projects she'd launched each year, involving her students in local history, folklore and traditions.

She caught a glimpse of sparkling water just off to the left. Last week's rains had produced some flooding in the low-lying fields adjoining the bay, and in the moonlight they were unbelievably beautiful. Durham was nice, but it wasn't on the Chesapeake.

For the hundredth time, her thoughts skittered over the question of whether or not to make the move—*if* they offered her the job. Before she could come to grips with that question, her flighty mind was off again, this time rehashing the romance she'd finished the night before.

Oddly enough, she'd enjoyed it. Priding herself on being objective, she was forced to admit that it was not nearly so well-written as the Jericho thing had been. All the same, she'd found herself quickly involved with the protagonists, empathizing with the heroine to an astonishing degree. The prose was a little too flowery for her tastes—a marked contrast to Jericho's work, which had a clean, direct style that was both terse and tender.

Recalling one of the more sensual passages, Emily's mind swerved back to Bey. She grimaced. Shoving the accelerator to the floor, she pulled out and passed a slow-moving chicken truck. Instead of fantasizing, she'd do well to apply herself to the problem of what to do between now and the opening term at St. Tommy's next August. Provided they wanted her.

Once through Easton, the countryside was dark. She hated driving at night, but at least the festival crowd had gone. She reminded herself that she still had a piece to write on that. She'd gone by the *Light* when she'd left the Gold Room, to hand over her notes in case Wendell was in a hurry. She hadn't made her plans at that point, but she'd known she had to get away. Wendell had handed her the bag of books and told her to get it in by Thursday for the Sunday edition. She hadn't argued. The extra money would come in handy, especially as she had no idea how she'd be able to support herself between teaching positions.

Turning into her driveway, she switched off the engine and slumped tiredly for a moment. The penetrating cold began to creep around her ankles as the effects of the asthmatic old heater quickly wore off. Somewhere she had to find the energy to go into the house before she fell asleep and caught pneumonia. Her bag could wait until tomorrow—no, it couldn't. She'd need her toothbrush. Oh, hell.

Opening the car door to the still, freezing air, she was reminded that her house would be cold and damp too. She hadn't taken time to lay a fire before she'd left, and she couldn't trust the furnace until she got around to getting it overhauled. The bathroom heater would have to serve, then. A hot soak, a glass of sherry, an electric blanket, in that order. School or no school, she'd postpone any really serious issues until tomorrow.

A shadow emerged from the deeper ones on her porch. Emily gasped and stepped back uncertainly. The shadow left the porch and moved toward her across the moonlit yard.

"It's about time you got home," Bey snarled, planting himself directly in her path. "Do you have any idea what I've been through since Saturday?"

"Bey? What's wrong?" Gone were all the indignation, all the jealousy and the anguish. Once more her mind was skittering around like a drunken butterfly, lighting on first one thing and then another: the substantial width of those leather-clad shoulders, the way they tapered so swiftly to a pair of narrow hips, the arrogant tilt of his head, the scent of woodsmoke that clung to him, enhancing the masculine aura she found so intoxicating.

Emily barely restrained herself from reaching out to him. By the time he touched her, she was shivering uncontrollably in the grip of a tension that had nothing at all to do with the frigid temperatures.

"Emily, Emily," he grated fiercely, pulling her into his arms to bury his face in her hair. "I ought to shake you until you rattle!"

Held prisoner in his powerful arms, she was helpless either to embrace him or to resist him. And for the life of her, she didn't know which she'd have done, given the chance.

"What are you doing here?" she managed finally, when she could get her face free of his throat. "Bey, is something wrong? Has something happened?" A kaleidoscope of possible disasters flickered through her mind and then it was gone, lost in the rush of more immediate considerations—like the feel of the rock-hard body that was all but supporting her, the scent of his flesh, the arms that held her as if they'd never let her go again.

"You're freezing," he muttered. "Hell, so am I. Let's get inside, and then you and I are going to do some talking. I can't go through another weekend like this again—God, woman, you're ruining my health, did you know that?"

A rough parody of a laugh emerged from his throat, and then Emily found herself being half-dragged to the front door. Bey waited impatiently until her fumbling fingers produced a key, and then he took it from her and rammed it home, his face almost obscured by the frosted vapor of his breath.

"My bag—my toothbrush," she protested weakly, and he pushed her inside.

"I'll get 'em."

The house was like a tomb. The scent of dead ashes and dead flowers assailed her nostrils as soon as she stepped inside. Moving stiffly, she began switching on lights. When Bey burst through the door again, dropping her bag to blow on his reddened knuckles, she was staring at the fireplace, trying to find the will to go out onto the back porch and bring in a load of wood. She wasn't even sure she had any kindling chopped.

"Let's get some heat in here," Bey growled, coming to stand behind her. "You turn up the thermostat and I'll get some firewood."

"The furnace needs a new dojigger. It just belches soot and then goes out."

"The fireplace'll do. Tell me where you keep your paper and kindling, and I'll get it going. Meanwhile, why don't you crawl under a blanket somewhere and

169

wait for me. We'll revive the old custom of bundling."
His grin went a long way toward thawing her out
before she caught herself.

"Newspapers in that copper boiler, firewood on the
back porch," she chattered, digging her hands into the
pockets of her coat. "You might have to split some
kindling. The hatchet's in the tool chest beside the
back door."

"Okay, you just sit tight, honey, and leave everything to me."

There was nothing she'd rather do, but certain
things took precedence, even over matters of the
heart. And the bathroom would be like an icebox until
the heater had had time to thaw it out.

At least the water heater worked. A few minutes
later, Emily stuck her head out the bathroom door.
"Bey? Look, I'm going to take a hot bath. It's either
that or dive headfirst under the electric blanket and
stay there until spring." The offhand cheerfulness was
surprisingly well done; she almost convinced herself.
"Stay as long as you like—get warm, make yourself
some coffee—and thanks for building me a fire. Just
be sure you put the fire screen in place before you
go."

By the time the tub was filled with steaming water,
the tiny bathroom was almost comfortable. Emily
peeled off the top layer of clothing. Amazing how
much cold could accumulate in a house that was
closed up for a few days. It was a good thing her pipes
were well insulated—she hadn't given a thought to
that sort of thing before she'd left.

One foot in the tub, she heard Bey's footsteps
approaching. She glanced apprehensively over her
shoulder. He wouldn't.

He would. "Hey—are you all right in there?"

The porcelain knob rattled suddenly and Emily hurriedly lowered herself into the green herbal-scented bathwater and jerked the shower curtain around the claw-footed tub.

"Of course I'm all right! Look, Bey, I'm really too tired to talk tonight. If you think we need to talk, then come back tomorrow after school—unless you're going back to Baltimore," she called through the white paneled door. If he headed a corporation, he must have to show up at an office *sometime.*

"Not on your life, lady. I didn't freeze my buns off all weekend just to build your fire. Tell me what clothes you want and I'll get 'em for you. I found your bathrobe and slippers in the bedroom. Anything else? Nightgown? Toothbrush?"

Emily closed her eyes, shaking her head in an effort to clear it. Things were piling up on her. It was all she could do to cope with one matter at a time, and she wasn't anywhere near ready to deal with Bey. Driving for hours alone, she'd given a lot of thought to the best way to extricate herself with the least possible damage to her ego. Never mind her heart—it was a hardier organ than the romance novels would have one think. At least she devoutly hoped it was.

"Emily? I'm not a particularly patient man." The knob rattled once more, underlining his pronouncement.

Doubling up her long legs, Emily slid under the water, puckering her mouth and eyes as it closed over her head. *Go away, dammit! Just go away and stop crowding me!*

Her eyes popped open again when she felt herself being lifted up by her hair. As the scented bath beads brought a wash of stinging tears to her eyes, she swore succinctly. "Dammit all to hell, will you just leave me—"

"No, I won't, and if you ever pull a damned fool stunt like that again, I'll turn you over my knee and whale some common sense into your aristocratic little backside!"

"My aristo . . . ! Bey, hand me a towel, will you? My eyes . . ." she wailed, pawing the air in the vicinity of the towel rack. Her hand collided with a leather-clad shoulder and then she felt her head being held in a viselike grip. A cool, damp cloth covered her burning eyes, and she groaned. Why was it that she always ended up behaving like a fool whenever he was around?

"There, my scrawny little mermaid, is that better?" The eyes were better—much better—but the amusement in that rasping drawl didn't do much for her composure. Besides which . . .

"Bey, will you get out of here?" Struggling against his superior strength, she flung aside the damp washcloth and jerked her head away from his hands. The clear plastic shower curtain wasn't much protection, but it was all she had. "Just get out," she ordered, glaring at him through red-rimmed eyes around a handful of plastic. He was kneeling there on her peach-colored bathmat, looking thoroughly intimidating in spite of the grin that crinkled his whole face. "Is this the way you get your kicks, preying on helpless females?"

"If you're helpless, then I'm a wooden Indian." Shrugging his massive shoulders, he slipped out of his coat.

"You're a *dead* one if you're not out of my house in one minute flat," she said malevolently, wrapping her arms around her chest. Her knees were drawn up until they brushed her chin, and her toes were curled defensively under the transparent green water.

Bey shoved up the sleeves of his shirt—an expensive-looking gray knit, she noticed distractedly. In fact, for once he was dressed in something other than jeans and boots. She found herself hotly resenting the fact that he was more attractive than ever. "Time's up," he murmured, amusement lacing his deep voice.

"Bey, please." She was drowning in those hazel eyes. By the time she felt herself going under for the third time, he'd reached into the tub for the washcloth she'd torn away from her eyes. "Why are you doing this to me?"

"What am I doing?" He soaped the cloth and placed a hand at the back of her dripping head.

"Badgering me. Hounding me." Her voice was muffled when the cloth covered the lower part of her face and then slipped down her throat.

"And don't you think you deserve it?" he asked in a tone of menacing reasonableness, caressing her throat with the fragrant suds as his supporting hand slipped down her back.

"I don't think anything," Emily moaned. "I don't know why you're here, I don't know why you're so angry—and you are, aren't you? That's why you're punishing me this way."

His head lowered, his voice drifting up to her ears in a cloud of scented steam. "Is this what you call punishment?" he asked just before his tongue flickered hotly over one tightly furled nipple. "And this?" He treated the other one to equal time, lifting its slight weight in a hard, soapy hand.

"You said you wanted to talk," Emily cried in a desperate attempt to regain control of the rapidly deteriorating situation. "Just let me get out of here and we'll talk!"

"I've changed my mind. I'm in no hurry to talk." One of his hands had dipped deeper into the water, in search of sunken treasure.

"Your sleeve's getting all wet. Bey—ah, please don't do that." She lowered her back against the high, sloping porcelain, helpless against the skill of his hands on her slippery skin.

"Tell me you don't like it and I'll stop," he rasped, raking his teeth over the sensitive tendon at the side of her neck.

"I . . ." The words lodged in her throat as his palm flattened on her body, spreading her thighs in a caress that rendered her completely boneless. Her head lolled like a heavy bud on a slender stalk. "Oh, please," she managed just before he lifted her from the water.

10

I'm getting you all wet," Emily protested distractedly as Bey held her up in his arms and plucked a towel from the rack. She was shivering almost uncontrollably, but not from the cold. The tiny room was steamy warm.

"I won't melt." Bey blotted her awkwardly while his lips drank the droplets from her cheeks, her eyes, her temples. "On second thought . . ." He lingered at the corner of her mouth for a moment too long, and then it was too late. Lowering her feet to the floor, he held her so tightly that she could feel his ribs pressing into the softness of her body.

"Ah, so sweet . . . so sweet," he whispered, melding his mouth to her parted lips to drink a sweeter nectar. With the hard palms of his hands, he raked the curve of her back, his fingertips tracing the shallow valley of her spine to hold her tightly to him.

Emily felt the galvanic response gathering deep inside her. Eagerly accepting his thrusting tongue, she gloried in the swift quickening of his taut body. She couldn't get close enough, couldn't touch enough, taste enough. The texture of his clothing, of his flat buckle, impressed itself on her skin, exciting her still further.

One of her feet lifted to rub the calf of her leg in slow, sensuous strokes as he closed his teeth gently over the point of her chin. When he began to nibble on her ear, tonguing the small pink aperture, she uttered a frenzied little whimper.

Her foot came down on the sleeve of his hastily shed coat, and she kicked it aside unheedingly. Her new coat, as well as the rest of her clothes, were down there somewhere—the least of her concern, at this point. Tugging his shirttail from the belt that circled his lean, flat waist, she struggled to remove it.

Freeing one arm at a time, Bey cooperated, never ceasing his ministrations to her ear, her throat, her tingling breasts. When his rumpled shirt joined the rest of the heap on the floor, Emily's hands moved in eager exploration from his back to his sides, to the wedge of dark hair that arrowed down to disappear under his belt.

"Here . . . please," he grunted, directing one hand to a tiny pointed nipple. "Ahhhh, swe-e-eet lightning!" he gasped.

Emily knew a fleeting moment of surprise at the intensity of her own pleasure when Bey shuddered and closed his eyes, the planes of his face oddly flattened by the force of his desire. She should be shocked at herself, at this glorious feeling of abandon that swept her along in its wake, but she wasn't. She wanted to do everything, to fuel the ravening fire in her own body by giving him all the pleasure there was.

"Like this?" she whispered tremulously, trailing her fingernails lightly over one of the small flat crowns that nestled in the crisp chest hair and then lowering her head to caress its mate with the tip of her tongue.

Bey's body jerked abruptly as he drew in a ragged breath. Something clattered to the floor—her body lotion. The room was incredibly cramped.

"Sweetheart, we've got to slow down," he grated hoarsely, catching both her hands in his and putting her away from him.

"But I don't want to slow down." Long past any hope of prudence, Emily twisted her damp wrists from his grip and reached for his buckle. She moved closer, backing him onto the cul-de-sac between the tub and the lavatory.

Eyes dark with desire, Bey made a valiant effort to regain his control, when the last thing on earth he wanted now was control. He'd been a fool even to touch her, but God! He wanted her so much it was crippling him. She wanted him, too—for now. But until things were settled, he couldn't risk it. If he couldn't have her for always, then he'd better start pulling out while he still had the courage.

"What happened to my inhibited, suppressed Miss Emily?" he whispered in a weak attempt to defuse the sexual tension between them. Raising his hands palms outward, he made a playful effort to fend her off.

Emily leaned forward. The placement was perfect. She could feel the rosy peaks of her breasts tighten into small pebbles as they snuggled into his hands.

"I'm much too tired to be inhibited." She lowered her face to his shoulder, smiling at the groan of defeat that rumbled in his throat. "Inhibitions take energy," she murmured. "I've had an incredibly tiring day."

"*You've* had a tiring day," Bey jeered softly. His arms closed around her once more and he brushed his open mouth over her lips—slowly, warmly, his moist, sweet breath mingling with hers. "Remind me to tell you a story someday."

His arms closed around her as he sighed heavily, and Emily realized that somehow the driving force of their desire had been transmuted into something less acute but just as warm. And it was all right. She leaned against him, feeling the weight of the last thirty-six hours settle upon her. Obviously Bey was a little wiser than she was. She'd have hated to fall asleep and miss the main feature.

"I think I'll quietly fall apart now," she informed him. "If you want to stay, you're welcome." Odd, the subtle differences in holding. The arms that had driven her wild only moments before were amazingly comforting now.

"I have no intention of leaving, sweetheart, but I think we could both do with some food." Bey felt his control wavering again, and he reluctantly put her from him. He was probably the world's biggest fool for not taking what she'd offered, but he had to be straight with her. Besides, he could use a shower, himself. The amenities on her front porch weren't all that great.

Reaching behind her, Emily felt for the doorknob. The inhibitions he'd accused her of arose swiftly as the colder air from the hall invaded the steamy warmth of the bathroom, reminding her of her nudity. "Ah . . . look, Bey, this was . . . I mean, if you don't mind . . ." Hopelessly she shook her head. Were there any social rules to cover a situation like this?

Her eyes pleaded with him, and it was all Bey could do not to drag her back inside the bathroom and carry on what he'd begun. Goosebumps on every inch of her flesh, wet hair plastered to her shoulders, she was still the most beautiful sight he'd ever seen.

He came to her rescue. "Look, if it wouldn't be too much trouble, I could really use some coffee and a shower. I've lived in these clothes all weekend."

Grasping the excuse he'd generously handed her, Emily stepped back, shivering as the draft struck her damp backside. "Me too. Look, I'll make coffee and scramble some eggs while you—"

"Great. Don't stint, will you? Confession might be good for the soul, but it's damned hard on the body. I'll need all the strength I can summon up."

"Confession?"

"Later," he promised tersely, reaching for the door and closing it gently in her face.

"Confession," Emily repeated softly to herself, turning slowly toward her bedroom across the hall. *"Confession?"*

The spurious energy her hot bath had restored began to ebb somewhere between the bedroom and the kitchen. Dressed in her best white silk pajamas and her warm quilted bathrobe, she measured coffee and set the automatic maker to working. She probably should have put on slacks and a sweater. Maybe she'd dash in and change before Bey came out. But first she'd get out the bacon.

By the time Bey emerged, she'd cooked a dozen slices of bacon and scrambled six eggs with cheese. She was still wearing her robe and pajamas, and her mind was beginning to run in circles again. After two all but sleepless nights and three hectic days, she was in no condition to deal with *confessions.*

Bey was going to tell her ever so diplomatically that he wasn't looking for any long-term commitment. Either that or he was married. Either that or he was involved with that Baltimore reporter. Or maybe both.

All she knew for certain was that he'd left her standing there in the middle of the Waterfowl Festival while he went off with Della two days earlier, and he'd been waiting here with his confession when she got home tonight. And dammit, if he turned out to be another Bo Edmonds, courting her while he had a wife and two children stashed away at home, she'd never *ever* forgive him! Nor forget him, she admitted miserably.

"Smells ambrosial," Bey murmured, coming up behind her as she dropped two slices of bread in the toaster and rammed down the lever. "Can we eat it in front of the fire?"

"What confession?" She turned and leveled a grim look at him, doing her very best to ignore the way her heart lurched at the sight of that strong, battered face.

"Later." Ignoring her scowl, he reached around her and snitched a slice of bacon from the paper towel on the counter.

"Bey, I'm serious. If you've got something that needs confessing, you'd better do it now, because I'm too tired to play guessing games."

"Honey, I understand—"

"You don't understand *anything,*" Emily insisted, deliberately allowing her anger to build into a defense against what was to come.

" 'Women are made to be loved, not to be understood.' Wasn't that Oscar Wilde?"

Crossing her arms, Emily glared at him. Her emotions had been on a roller coaster long enough; the ride was over. "Stop *quoting* at me! You're so damned glib until I ask you a straight question, and then all I get is evasions!"

"Patience, darlingest Emily. 'A noble man is led far by woman's gentle words.' "

"Noble, my foot. You want a quote? I'll quote you a quote! I'm not an English teacher for nothing. 'Being a woman is a terribly difficult trade, since it consists largely of dealing with men.' "

"Touché. You're a worthy opponent, Miss Emily. I foresee some dandy matches between us. Do you like *Hamlet?*"

Her mouth fell open. Behind her, the toast popped up and began to cool. *"Hamlet?"*

Willing himself the courage to tell her, Bey took a deep breath. He'd quoted *Hamlet* in one of those letters signed B.J. It was as good an opening as any. His courage wavered. "On second thought, forget *Hamlet.* Maybe I'd better drag out *The Merchant of Venice,* for that thing about the quality of mercy."

Confusion shadowed Emily's pale features. "Bey, I think you'd better stop hiding behind other people's words and level with me."

They were standing so close he could see the fear growing in her eyes. Good God, what did she think he was going to confess, bank robbery? Tax evasion?

Growing more miserably self-conscious by the moment, he began to quote from the final scene of *Reap the Wild Wind.* " 'And when she'd pierced his soul through the window of his eyes, there was no place to hide. Neither of them spoke. No words were needed to express the love that had been there from the beginning of time.'" He waited, feeling his heart expand in fear, his mouth go dry. "Those are my words, Emily. Don't you recognize them?"

Firelight flickered softly on the haphazardly stacked dishes. Bey reached for the half-slice of bacon she'd left on her plate, and Emily divided the last of the coffee. "Publishing. That was slightly misleading, you know. I was beginning to wonder why you never seemed to spend any time in the office. Do you know that I thought you were a land developer at first?"

They were lying under a creamy woolen blanket, feet to the fire, shoulders brushing. One of Emily's slippered feet was captured by both of Bey's bare ones and squeezed gently. "That's a hug," he confided. "I didn't really want to mislead you—well, maybe just at first. I was really ticked off when I read your review."

Emily slapped her Wedgwood cup carelessly into its saucer and groaned. "Oh, Lord, don't remind me. And those letters—I'm amazed you didn't tar and feather me under the circumstances. And all that time, you *knew*."

He shrugged, and when his arm encountered hers, he rearranged it so that it cradled her head. "In case you forgot, Emily McDarling, I said a few less-than-flattering things about you, too. Of course, I soon saw the error of my ways."

She turned to face him, her gaze caressing the marvelous irregularities of his profile as he stared up at the ceiling. "It wasn't *how* you wrote, you know—it was *what* you wrote. I thought you were fostering totally unrealistic hopes in susceptible young women, and it struck me as awfully unfair. I thought I was an expert on love, of course." Her soft laughter was colored with the faintest shade of bitterness. "I didn't know the first thing about it. My sophomores knew more than I did."

Silence stretched out between them. Nothing had been said about love—not in so many words. Bey had told her everything, from his early days as an escapee from various foster homes and orphanages, to his army career and the turning point that had come in the veterans' hospital when he'd read his first romance.

She, in turn, had told him about her parents and Libby and Vangie. He'd grunted when she'd got to Wendell, and she'd tactfully left out both Bo and Jonathan. They were, she sincerely hoped, in the same category as the women in his past, women like Della Brame.

After a while Bey said, "I have trouble saying it. That's ironic, isn't it? I can put the words into the mouths of my heroes and my heroines, but I can't speak the lines to save me." He turned to her then, his eyes glowing with an unmistakable message.

"So put it in a book," Emily whispered, reaching up to trace the laugh line in his lean cheek.

"How about a modern version of *Beauty and the Beast?*"

"How about a modern version of *Prince Charming and the Witch?*"

"How about we collaborate on the timeless story of Mr. and Mrs. Jones?"

Emily could hardly speak past the constriction in her throat. A tremulous smile was born on her lips, and it quickly spread into a broad, contagious grin. "I wish I had some champagne—something special."

"I'll order us a case tomorrow. What do you like, French? New York? California?"

She reached across him to replace her cup on the hearth. "Anything. Everything. Bey, why didn't you tell me sooner?"

Scooping more pillows from the sofa, he made a nest of them and resettled them, pulling her over so that she sprawled across his chest. "Do you have any idea of the sort of courage it takes for a man to tell a woman he writes romances? Especially when that woman has gone on record as despising the whole genre?" His square-tipped fingers smoothed the hair from her temple and he brushed a kiss along the curve of her cheekbone. "Especially," he added ruefully, "when the man isn't exactly noted for his romantic appearance."

"Have you any idea how much courage it takes for a woman to admit that she was wrong? I think I was afraid of discovering how much I was missing, Bey." The fire crackled noisily as he slipped her arms from her robe and pulled the blanket over her silk-clad shoulders. "You don't know how much courage it takes for a woman to be alone when she's no longer very young. Not to live alone—but to be alone."

He held her close, inhaling the clean fragrance of her hair, her skin. "I know, I know," he crooned, touching her face as if it were the delicate petal of a lotus. "I know about being alone. I know about emptiness, but no more, love." He kissed her eyes shut. "No more."

"It makes no sense at all, you know," she protested

feebly when his fingers released the last button on her shirt. "I don't even know how to ride a motorcycle."

"All you have to know how to do is hold me. Would you care to start practicing now?" Sitting up, he stripped off his shirt and tossed it aside. Shining his crooked smile down on her, he muttered, "That's the trouble with this time of year—too many clothes. Do you suppose togas would be too impractical for Maryland winters?"

She helped him with his trousers, and then he made short work of removing her pajamas. "You're much too young for me, you know," she reminded him. "I'll be accused of all sorts of wicked things."

"I certainly hope so." He removed a leaf that had stuck to her hip. "Have you raked your living room lately?"

"You tracked that in. And anyway, I never claimed you could eat off my floors."

"It wasn't exactly eating I had in mind," Bey pointed out. He gave up on trying to keep them covered, and rolling her over onto her back, began the task of warming her with his body.

"Bey, do you think you could manage to support us both while I did some postgraduate work? There's so much I missed out on."

He traced the circulation of her inner arm with a series of inflammatory kisses. "Hmmmm, might join you, darling. I missed one or two things myself."

"Emily," he murmured sometime later, "you understand that I don't have any background—no family, I mean? If I had any ancestral portraits at all, they were probably the type exhibited at post offices."

Emily lifted her hands to his face, touching one of the faint scars on his chin. "It occurs to me that I'd much rather *be* an ancestor than have any number of them," she said thoughtfully.

Bey paid homage to one small ripe breast and then the other. Lifting his head, he gazed down at her slumberous eyes. "I think I might be able to help out with a quest like that, McDarling."

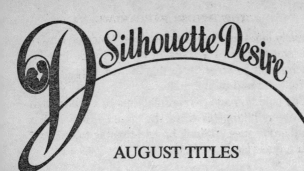

Silhouette Desire

Silhouette Desire

COMING NEXT MONTH

A DIFFERENT REALITY
Nora Powers

It didn't take long before his dark eyes and whimsical imagination had her head spinning until she wasn't sure where the border between fantasy and reality lay. But while Kerr's fantasies were truly fantastic, his feelings were passionately real. Or were they…?

A WOMAN OF INTEGRITY
Marie Nicole

Chyna O'Brien was a stuntwoman, a professional risk taker. Maybe Matt really *did* feel something for her. Finding out was going to be the most dangerous move of her career.

GOLDEN MAN
Ann Major

Having Blade around stirred feelings Jenny feared. His golden looks and the vivid memory of an afternoon they'd once shared were enough to set her heart ablaze all over again…

COMING NEXT MONTH

CATTLEMAN'S CHOICE
Diana Palmer

No other woman dared approach him. And even Mandelyn soon began to wonder whether a few lessons in manners could ever make a gentleman of an outlaw like Carson Wayne.

HUNGRY FOR LOVE
Ariel Berk

Wealthy, self-made, Wes was a curious mixture of street tough and tender lover, straightforward… honest. Though they came from opposite backgrounds, they both had the same thing to prove, the same needs: a hunger for love.

JOURNEY TO DESIRE
Laurie Paige

Tender, provocative Mark Terrington seemed bent on learning her secrets, even as he remained strangely distant. Had she fallen in love with the man of her dreams, or a dangerous enemy who was after her mind, not her heart?

Four New Silhouette Romances could be yours ABSOLUTELY FREE

Did you know that Silhouette Romances are no longer available from the shops in the U.K?

Read on to discover how you could receive four brand new Silhouette Romances, **free** and **without obligation,** with this special introductory offer to the new Silhouette Reader Service.

As thousands of women who have read these books know — Silhouette Romances sweep you away into an exciting love filled world of fascination between men and women. A world filled with

age-old conflicts — love and money, ambition and guilt, jealousy and pride, even life and death.

Silhouette Romances are the latest stories written by the world's best romance writers, and they are **only** available from Silhouette Reader Service. Take out a subscription and you could receive 6 brand new titles every month, plus a newsletter bringing you all the latest information from Silhouette's New York editors. All this delivered in one exciting parcel direct to your door, with no charges for postage and packing.

And at only 95p for a book, Silhouette Romances represent the very best value in Romantic Reading.

Remember, Silhouette Romances are **only** available to subscribers, so don't miss out on this very special opportunity. Fill in the certificate below and post it today. You don't even need a stamp.

- - - - - - - - - - - - - - - - ✂ - - -

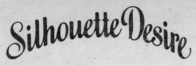

Silhouette Desire

Your chance to write back!

We'll send you details of an exciting free offer from *SILHOUETTE*, if you can help us by answering the few simple questions below.

Just fill in this questionnaire, tear it out and put it in an envelope and post today to: Silhouette Reader Survey, FREEPOST, P.O. Box 236, Croydon, Surrey CR9 9EL. You don't even need a stamp.

What is the title of the *SILHOUETTE Desire* you have just read?

_____

How much did you enjoy it?

Very much ☐   Quite a lot ☐   Not very much ☐

Would you buy another *SILHOUETTE Desire* book?

Yes ☐   Possibly ☐   No ☐

How did you discover *SILHOUETTE Desire* books?

Advertising ☐   A friend ☐   Seeing them on sale ☐

Elsewhere (please state) _____

How often do you read romantic fiction?

Frequently ☐   Occasionally ☐   Rarely ☐

Name (Mrs/Miss) _____

Address _____

_____

_____ **Postcode** _____

Age group: Under 24 ☐   25–34 ☐   35–44 ☐
                 45–55 ☐   Over 55 ☐

Silhouette Reader Service, P.O. Box 236, Croydon, Surrey CR9 9EL.
Readers in South Africa—write to:
Silhouette Romance Club,
Private Bag X3010, Randburg 2125.

SD1